I0708523

The Don in Heels: the Inner Thoughts of thee Minnie Mogul

The Don in Heels: the Inner Thoughts of thee Minnie Mogul

By K.T. Braxton

ISBN 979-8-218-41103-9

Dedication

Mommy and Daddy, I can never repay you but I'm going to try for the rest of my days. Thank you for the unconditional love, the work ethic, the wisdom, the strength, everything. I love you more than I could ever say.

To my only begotten sister, I love you forever.

To my loved ones absent from the body and present with the King of Kings, I hope I'm making you proud. If no one else thought I would be somebody my granddaddy did, so I shall live each day trying to prove him right.

This book would not be a reality without my ROD, creative bestie, and editor. Thank you, Tiffani DuPree. Cheers to us and our labor of love! Thank you for everything.

To the man I didn't know I could dream of, thanks for the journey and the lessons. I'm always rooting for you. I love you forever and always.

To the stranger this is meant for, I dedicate this to you. I'm a relatively private person, so writing this was arduous. I walk the very thin line of keeping my private life private while still being transparent. I'm translucent. *Yeah, that feels right.* Some people will judge me because of the content. Some people may laugh. Others might cry. I hope some will learn something, but I know a piece of the small pie of readers will simply ask "Who cares?" and that's alright. I asked God "Why am I to write this book?" I said, "I'm nobody." He told me "Write," so I wrote. So cheers to the readers who God chose to eat of the words from the depths of my soul. May you be blessed.

Anotha

October 18, 2021

Thank you, Lord, for waking me up this morning. Welp, I suppose I'm up; it's 4 o'clock in the morning. I just want to sleep in, but who am I kidding? Okay, let's take inventory: be on set by 8am, get to the café by 4pm, and I have to remember to check on the offices tomorrow. Alright let me get it together. I guess I'll get a head start on my routine, then reply to some pressing emails before getting ready for the day.

...

"Ma'am, we're ready for you." *The sound guy is so formal and... wayment! Do I look old enough to be a MA'AM?!* "I'm coming, thank you," I reply, returning back to the excitement of finally seeing my dream of having a cooking talk show! Seriously, I get paid to cook, talk, sing, and have random dance breaks! That is incredible to me. *Suckas, I would have done it for free.* I can't help but have a Grinch-like grin on my face. *Okay, it's almost time. I can't believe I'm on television. Oh Lawd...Breathe girl, just breathe. You got this.* I silently repeat one of my favorite sayings until go-time. *Poppin. Poppin. Poppin.*

"5. 4. 3. 2..."

"Heeyyy everybody, welcome to Faith &
Food. Today while we get to know each
other we are making spinach tarts with
phyllo dough, my take on Beef Wellington,
grilled asparagus with a deliciously
simple white wine butter sauce, roasted
purple potatoes, and last but not least red
velvet cake! Who doesn't like cake?
People who don't like happiness that's
who!" As the audience cheers, I hope they
can't tell how nervous I am.

...

Mmmm my favorite, red velvet cake! I can still
smell it from all the way upstairs. The layers of
the cake used to always stick to the pans except
for when she made it for no one other than me!
Yeah, the cake chose me. Sometimes I still get
glimpses of the day she taught me how to make it.
It's not the clearest of memories, but I remember
the sun brightening the big kitchen with ample
counter space. I was just barely tall enough to see
over it. Once I felt the power of the mixer, saw
how everything came together, and understood
that order does matter, I never turned back;
nothing was the same anymore.

My grandmas didn't teach me a whole lot in the
kitchen, outside of my paternal grandma teaching

me how to bake that cake when I was around 10 years old. I had helped bake Christmas cookies long before that, but that cake is the only one of two vague memories I have of Mama actually teaching me one-on-one. Granny, my maternal grandma, wasn't always kid-friendly and teaching wasn't her thing. Ironically in her final year, she was convinced that she was a teacher because of her overflowing love for children. Dementia is something else.

My mom showed me how to clean greens some time ago, then I became the designated greens maker of the family. When she walked out the kitchen, it was just me and the pot minding our business and I secretly added more spices. When the greens were ready, along with my secret additions, everyone raved about "Mommy's" greens. I kept it in but later told my sister. That day was a precursor to me finding and accepting my true love in the kitchen. Naysayers have tried to take away from this art by which I bear my soul by insinuating that I got to where I am now off trial and error, not innate ability. I choose to see it as a reminder of growth. Look where I am now. I get paid to cook on tv. I wasn't formally trained, but I was still chosen for this. I haven't arrived yet, but I've had enough confirmation to accept that this gift I have benefits more than just me. I had to hone-in on skills to get to this point and I'll keep learning and growing as everyone should, but these instincts came from the depths of my soul. My parents are very supportive and have been all my life, but out of all my gifts, cooking was nurtured the least because we were not rich. There weren't free culinary programs for kids like me where I come from, or at least they weren't advertised; plus food costs money! I couldn't really experiment until I could pay for my own groceries. I've literally put my money where my mouth is.

...

After wrapping up my first taping in front of a small audience, I coast through the city I've always known, and my mind goes adrift. I'm suddenly nostalgic thinking of the way things were, the ups and downs, and what is still to come. Detroit has resilience written all over the place *even though sometimes it gives very much gentrification*. I suppose it was a befitting place to grow, to evolve. I was born in the jungle, and I ain't even know. I knew there were areas not to go to, I wasn't oblivious; I just ain't grow up in the hood. My parents worked hard to shelter my sister and me from a lot and I'm grateful for that. Seeing the city through other people's experiences as an adult hits differently. That doesn't mean I didn't have struggles, but the ones they could shield me from they did and that's why I see the beauty in where I'm from where some people see filth. Some who experienced living here differently only saw a place to get out of and never return. I can understand that.

Before I know it, I'm lost in the music. My eclectic library goes from Selena to Fall Out Boy to New Edition to Luther Vandross. Before I even realize, my trivial thoughts come to a close as I am pulling up to the café, "Kenny's Kitchen," but first I need a get-out-song. I always need the perfect song to end my car ride, something to set the tone. I settled on a classic, "Gotta Move" by Barbra Streisand.

Oh, I'm goofy, I should probably introduce myself. Hi, I am who some call 'Thee Minnie Mogul' because of my various business pursuits while others tend to call me 'The Don in Heels,' which might be my favorite as I am around 5'5 to 5'7, but without my heels I stand tall at 5'2. Really, I go by many names, but my friends call me Kenny.

The place was PACKED for a Monday evening, and I was here for it, but goodness gracious I am grateful to finally be closing for the night. I am what you call ti'ed! As I get home, I try to decompress and review my schedule for the rest of the week. In a couple of days, I have a business trip, but my sister is going to meet me in LA and we're going to have sista-time. *"It's sista-time! It's sista-time,"* So what? I talk to myself and

annoyingly mock my sister in a reality tv
personality's voice!

Heading home, I can't help but think that I
actually built the home of my dreams. I didn't
imagine I would do it alone, but I'm grateful. I
remember walking through praying at each stage
of building. I wanted to fill my house with love,
peace, and power, laying a foundation to make it
a home before adorning the house with fabulous
furnishings. It's still so brilliantly strange to me
that my dreams are coming to fruition.

As I get close to home, my phone buzzes and it's
Mia Gina Jenkins. She's congratulating me on the
house completion and to remind me that we
graduated about ten years ago. *I know it ain't
been that long fa ya girl.*

> "You seeing all this stuff about ten-year
> reunions?" Mia casually asks.
> "Yeah, it's so odd. Ten years. It's like we
> blinked and boom we getting up there"
> "I know! But some days, it still seems like
> just yesterday…"
> "Straight up, but I'm pretty sure I ain't
> goin" I slide that in nonchalantly.
> "Mmm, you thought"
> "Fa real, I legit may not go"
> "You're going!" She exclaims.

"Gimme one good reason!"

She tries to give me cliché responses and with no preamble she asks, "Have you talked to him?"

"No, it's been 2 or 3 years now," I say unaffected to her surprise.

I haven't thought about the infamous *him* of my adolescence in some time. Mia and I chat a little while longer catching up with one another before we both decide to retire for the evening. We haven't talked in so long, but it was like no time was missed. Before she moved, whenever I would go out, it was with her. Growing up is crazy. I don't remember the last time I went out for a good time at all.

...

It's morning again. I get ready for my day; I have to go to my meeting with the suppliers and check on the offices. Even though Kenny's Kitchen is where I am most present, the days when it is closed or when I let my sous chef, Michele, handle things, "*BARELY!!,*" my subconscious roars at me. *OKAY! Try to let my sous chef handle things,* I am able to focus on the other businesses within Braxton Holdings Incorporated. I check in often, plus I stay in constant communication with my managers. Unlike many founders, I am still very hands on. I don't have a board; I own my corporation entirely. I stay determined to keep pushing forward and protecting the image of all the entities within it because I'm a Kingdompreneur, meaning that how I move in business should still reflect that I'm a child of God. My employees, clients and such don't necessarily have to be Christians for me to work with them, but I don't hide Jesus. The boardroom naturally isn't the place for a sermon, but how I operate in business is based on my values, morals, and ethics all stemming from my faith in the Most High. I try to treat folks how I want to be treated and understand that some elements, even in business, should be above money. It doesn't mean I'm supposed to be all passive and let folks walk all over me. God gifted me, I've done the work, got credentials and experience, so I don't work for free unless I volunteer or it's straight ministry *or my parents volunteer me. I don't think they'll ever stop doing that.* I choose to live my life striving to be pleasing to God in all I do. It doesn't mean I get everything right, but it means I put in the effort.

Whew chile, am I trying today? Some of these folks with my suppliers are working my last nerve. *Lord, please cover me.* In between meetings and scheduled conference calls, I check my phone and respond based on priority level, so naturally, I call my sister back first and I look forward to the brief reprieve.

"Hey CoCo, what's up?"

"Nothin' Kenny. Just checkin' in. Tomorrow's the big day. I can't wait to see you."

"I know, me neither. It will be a nice break."

"Yes! You and I both need a vacay, Sishur!"

"You said that right on time! Sorry Sis, I'm gonna be late fa my next meeting. If I don't talk to you tonight, I'll see you in LA! You're my half-sister, but I whole love you!"

"Love you too, Step-Sister! See you tomorrow!"

...

 My goal was never to be wealthy or even rich, but I must say flying private is mad dope. One of my closest friends, Shawn, is a pilot. *I love knowing the right people...I couldn't afford this.* Fortunately, the flight has been pretty smooth, but my thoughts are a bit turbulent. Suddenly, I find myself thinking of a couple years ago when we went on a sister trip to Portland to see our cousin, Bebe. We had a huge blow up...I blew up. In our own life stories, we're respectively the protagonist, maybe even heroine, but in one another's we've all too often been the antagonist. We innately rile up one another. I guess that's the thing with siblings, but whenever we needed each other, for each other is what we were.

Honestly, I cannot even remember exactly what was said that made me go off, but it was as if the levee just broke, and the water was boiling. It was not like the years prior-which led to me getting a punching bag-this was the mother of all blow-ups, as in the make or break of our sisterhood. I slightly cringe and sit unsettled in my seat just thinking about it. She set me off like just about no one could or can... I was so tired of accepting the role of the villain. I had held my tongue for long enough and I was over it.

> "You've spoken enough! It's my turn now. You always act like I was Satan's spawn and you were the Angel. I'm tired of it. I can accept my faults. I can't change the past. I can admit that I wasn't a good kid, but what you not gone do is make it seem like I'm all bad and you're all good then take credit for who I've become or what I've built! You were SUPPOSED to be an example, but you often provoked me instead of encouraging me or leaving me the hell alone, you poked a bear. I'm not gonna pretend like it was always that way, but you never even admitted that many times we argued because you wouldn't LEAVE ME ALONE! You are not

my mother. All my life, you've wanted respect from me that you did not earn. I do everything I can to show you that I love you and will do just about anything for you, including die for you, but I'm tired of this and I will no longer tolerate it. If you wanna continue this, I guess I'll just see you when it involves Mom and Dad."

That day after I went off, I walked away. I had to go someplace to calm down and pray because I was too hot and had met my limit. Later when I saw Bebe, CoCo was there, and I was left to assume that she chose to move forward. We speak regularly and we have never spoken of that incident, not once. Hopefully it stays that way. This is the first sister trip we're taking since then…

Finally, I have arrived. The smooth halt of the plane has ceased my unruly thoughts. Not too long after, my sister and I were reunited. Today, we're hitting the spa 'cause we deserve it. My sister is the big shot at this fancy resort in Arizona. Occasionally, when I'm in a crunch I contract her as a consultant to train my café staff. Many people wonder why we don't work together more. The answer is simply because I value our relationship too much. We are very similar but also very different, which is why we've clashed so much over the years. We are our parents' children. Tomorrow, we are going to have a day on the town and if we aren't too tired we may go to a lounge. I'm on Operation: Find a Brotha-In Law.

Chillin' by the pool, CoCo and I take in the scenery while I'm plottin'. We exchange sisterly banter, philosophies, and jokes that are likely considered wildly inappropriate.

> "You just mad my momma and daddy still together and you come from a broken home!" I say sticking my tongue out.
> "You ole stout out cow!" She quips as Danielle rings my phone.
> "Simple Jack! You here?"
> "Yeah nigga"
> "Iight we on the way. CoCo, we gotta go get yo cousin."

My parents were married, had CoCo, separated, divorced, remarried, and had me. One night my mom jokingly had a revelation. She said to me "CoCo is from my first marriage and you're from my second marriage." Let's just say I took it and ran with it. CoCo is my half, step, and whole sister.

Before I know it, we are singing in the elevators, making scenes, and exchanging insiders in front of mixed company. It takes me back to all of us kickin' it on the kitchen floor at the old house. Our grandparents' house. Actually, the previous owner left it to my dad when she passed. Daddy always looked out for everyone, which is why Danielle is really more like a sister to CoCo and me. She's an only child and after her mom, Tee, passed away she became even more like our sister.

This mini getaway is exactly what I needed, but I am so exhausted. Suddenly, I am pulled back into reality after an awesome night out of kickin' it with my family. While we wind down, I check emails. Before I open the business matters, I see some messages from some of my mentees from the church and outreach initiatives. It's really as though they teach me more than I do them. *I know one thing they sho do teach ya girl patience.* They are some beautiful souls waiting to love and be loved. I have family dinners for them at my house every couple of months so they can build a network within each other. Mommy always said I should be a teacher. I suppose I have blossomed into the teacher she prophesied me to be. *Lord, why do you always talk to me through her?*

We spend our last couple days exploring and absorbing some culture before being thrown back into the hustle and bustle. I don't always realize how much I miss being around them until I've seen them and then have to depart. When I get home, I am overwhelmingly blissful because the first recording of the show is ready for me to watch. I think I'm going to have a watch party. I can't even view it right now, so I instead jump back into work mode to calm my nerves.

…

On my way to the headquarters, I'm optimistic. My right hand, Meaghan, is on it and I typically have her on projects for every entity in the corporation. Oh man, that reminds me I have to hire a new assistant. The one I have is wonderful, but she's accepting a huge opportunity to go to South Carolina. Haley is the sweetest, but I believe in growth. I'm glad we served as a stepping stone for her, and based on the rapport we've established I don't doubt that we'll see more of each other.

Some of my weeks are all over the place. I might not know if I'm coming or going, so that's why I acknowledge my need for a strong team and I try to show my appreciation. I can't do everything I do without them. We're all needed to keep this train movin'.

Shucks! I need to draw up some more NDAs for the prospective newcomers. I mean I'm not into any kind of freaky-deaky stuff or anything like that, but I value privacy. My team often sees what most don't, and I have some things I like to keep to myself...

Some would call it a secret, though it's not very well kept. I call it private information. Others know something is up, but have no details. Typically, only those in my inner circle truly know; there are few exceptions. You can't see it, except for when I have really bad days or I'm caught slippin'. For some, it's out of sight, out of mind. The fact remains I'm sick. I fight my body on a daily basis. Yes, the saved one who believes firmly in healing. Yes, the minister who preaches and teaches, who prays for people, tarrying on their behalf seeing God's hand touching their lives. I know I'm healed whether I see God manifest it on this side or the other. Most days it does not show and the days that it does I work to remain unseen. I know we were created to be spiritual beings, and this is just a natural experience, but right now we live in a natural reality and being chronically ill is a part of mine...

Healing is such a huge topic, especially in the Christian faith. Everybody's journey is different. Some people see a miraculous healing here on earth, some are called to His presence early and put out of agony. Others have faith that whether they see a physical healing on this side or the next, they know that their spiritual healing has taken place and they'll take steps to ensure that process continues. Kinda like myself. Whatever ails me doesn't belong to me because I know Who is in control. I don't doubt the power of God because I've seen it before too many times not to believe it. I know that we were all equipped with different gifts and volumes thereof. I suppose one of my gifts is strength because I'm still standing. Sometimes people say things just because they sound good, and that is why it is imperative to know God for yourself or you'll always be caught in the winds of people's fleeting words. At times, it is frustrating with people trying to lay hands and say "you're healed you'll wake up with no more sickness." Shucks, sometimes they're worse than the actual sickness. I just wanna tell 'em like my Golden Girl Sophia said, "You're starting to annoy me. You shouldn't annoy a sick person." *For one, everybody can't lay hands on me 'cause everybody's spirit ain't right and oftentimes what they say isn't even sound.*

Because of my human nature, some days are tough, and at times I feel like I'm losing. During stupors and excessive bouts of being bedridden, my mind wanders, craziness tries to take over or maybe it's also loneliness. I can't help but think: how can I ever be the fabulous wife and mother I aspire to someday be? *Well, when I'm ready of course...* I mean I'm a dope chick, but the reality of the situation is that in the natural I don't always look too dope. I am in my late twenties and use a cane some days. That ain't hot! What can I do for someone other than bring strife? Some days I can't walk, and that kinda crawling ain't sexy. *Well, not that I'm out here tryna get sexy fa a playa, but ya know what that ain't e'en the point.*

My phone goes off and instantly a smile comes to my face...
> "Hey Mommy, how you doin' girlfriend?"
> "I'm okay, baby girl. What's wrong?" She could hear the sheer discomfort in my voice I tried so hard to mask.
> "Nothing Momma. I'm just tired."
> "How about I come by today? Your dad is at a golf outing, so we can have a movie day."
> "That sounds perfect."

Apparently, I am forever five. No matter how grown I am, I still love a day with Mommy. We have a beautiful co-dependent relationship; *it's lowkey borderline problematic but whatever.* My parents have been fighting this battle nearly as much as I have over these years. Sometimes I reflect on my lack of an abundance of friends, though I was raised to want quality friends not quantity. While other people were forging lifelong friendships and cultivating relationships during teenage and young adult years, I was home sick or needed a part-time caregiver.

Not long after we hang up, I hear my mom pull into the driveway. She uses her key to let herself in, "Hey, where are you?" "I'm upstairs!" My mom walks upstairs and enters my room with some of my favorite snacks. "Thanks Mommy! You always know how to make me feel better. I couldn't make it down the stairs today yet." After Jesus, Mommy has been my rock.

In my formidable years, Momma used to hang out with me on really bad days when I was basically held hostage by my own body. My parents did everything they could for me, but they never wanted me to work too hard because of these constraints. I knew I was not going to live with them forever and I always knew that one day I wanted to take care of them. Because of that, I feverishly work when I can because I never know when I can't, plus I enjoy the work I do. I'm living out my purpose.

My mom is really the only safe space I have where I can truly be not okay. She gets the good, bad, and immensely ugly, whilst others may only get a glimpse of pretty ugly.

"Last week was pretty good. I was able to get through everything. We finished a few projects at the offices, the apparel line is doing well, the kitchen is running smoothly, I had an interview for a new assistant, and I did a few tapings for the show."

"Sweetie, when are you going to slow down? You're only one person. I know how gifted you are and how God has entrusted you with a lot, but don't you think you have too much on your plate?"

"I know it sounds like a lot, but all this week my body has not allowed me to get much of anything done. I work so hard because I never know when I can't. 'To whom much is given, much is required.' I try not to add too much, but I was given too much not to work hard. I know at times I may push the limits a little too far. I gotta work on it, but Daddy always told me not to let a little pain stop me."

"This is more than just a little pain. I just want you to be careful. Don't speed up the time God gave you; your dad and I are still waitin' on grandkids!" *And here we go. Really not in the mood for where this is headed. Jesus, please be my strength.*

"Mom, can we not today? Y'all have been ready for grandkids for Lord knows how long. Y'all treat me like an old spinster."

She laughs and then has the audacity to pretend like I'm lyin'... *Apparently I'm not enough because I have no man and haven't popped out kids yet. Somehow she'll turn this around to wanting me to be happy, I'm sure.*

"We do not treat you like a spinster! We just want some babies around. Besides, you will make a great little mommy."
"Mommy you've been saying that since I was a teenager."
"Well it's true. Of course, we want you to get married first. We want to see you happy and with someone. You deserve to be happy and have someone who will be there for you and take care of you especially in times like this." *Yup, and we arrived. If it wasn't already my money, I'd bet myself money.*
"Well Momma, I'm doing the best I can. I'm just beginning to learn how to love myself, and I can't meet a man on bedrest!"
"I know, but maybe if you work a little less, you'd be able to meet someone"
"Mom, I love you, but I can't do this today. I thought you were coming to help me feel better..."
"I'm sorry, I didn't mean to upset you"

While she's still here, we try to salvage the day and change the subject. We land on Nollywood films and order food. I was hoping for playful banter, not a reminder that I'm inadequate. I have a fulfilling life overall. I've worked my butt off to be self-sufficient so that I don't depend on my parents as much. I have built my home to fit my needs whether I'm blessed to be a wife and mom or not. Though Mommy has been a part of this fight in many ways, she still doesn't profoundly understand because this isn't her story. Having children might be a little bit more complicated for me...

As the night fell, Mommy left after I adamantly assured her that I would be okay. I'm tuckered out, drifting in and out of sleep, but my mind keeps spiraling. Sometimes it's exasperating how conversations with Mommy can do that. So, maybe I'm not much of a dater? I don't like excessive or stupid questions. I don't like vulnerability. In fact, I just might loathe it, and I am ultra guarded because of my health. I don't want to sit here and pretend like I'm all lonely and that's all I think about because that would be a bald-faced lie, but the thought crosses my mind especially on days like this-here alone in my primary bedroom in this big ole house. I don't just want a wedding. I want a marriage, a thriving and successful marriage, so this husband would have to understand me and motivate me to be a good wife, the perfect one for him, his rib, his helpmate. Something about him would have to convince me to show him everything I got, the good, the bad, the ugly, without shame. I'm not gone rush that because if I'm blessed enough for it to happen, I pray it lasts. I don't want to be a burden to anyone else. Getting married would be the biggest decision of my life, after choosing Jesus, because we would truly be sharing life in every way.

The first time I had an asthma attack alone in the shower, I was terrified. It was years ago at the family house. I was there so my mom could look after me during the exacerbation, but she was all the way on the other side of the house. She couldn't hear me. I cried because it dawned on me "I could die like this. All alone with no one to hear me." I thought when my parents are no longer here, will anyone care? Will I have done enough? Will I have accomplished enough? Will I have been a good enough person, a good enough servant of God? Though this was so chilling, and I didn't want to be alone, I knew I never wanted anyone to be there because they had to be. I don't want to have children just to force someone to take care of me in my old age if I'm blessed to get old. Yes, I pray I have kids, love them unconditionally and do a good enough job that when I am old they want to be around me. It took a miracle to get me out of that shower to my room to get my inhaler then administer my treatments. That Storybrooke disease thoroughly affects my quality of life, especially coupled with intermittent breathing troubles, but even still it's not like I have cancer or anything like that, so I don't even know if someone would take it seriously.

More importantly, I have to take into account who I am as a woman and be honest about my own flaws. I am very much Walt and Nita's child. In many ways, I'm more like my father in the best and worse ways, but nonetheless Nita is still very evident. I have his sarcasm, his ability to not care and be removed, his lack of emotional investment, his tendency to be controlling, and his temper. Outbursts that have scared others didn't phase me and that's lowkey scary. On the good foot, I have his sense of humor and storytelling, his commitment to responsibility, his loyalty, his strength, and his leadership. Like him, when I love, I truly love. Like my mother, I'm teachable but have a tendency to be autocratic. I like to think I can walk into any room and relate like her. When I am invested, I give it all I got and sometimes have a hard time saying no like her. I can be understanding and empathetic, but can also make excuses for people when I deserve better. Though she wants better for me in many ways, much of what she hopes for me I have never seen. Growing up in a nuclear family does not mean I had the perfect, picturesque family. I did not grow up seeing thriving marriages, so when I see them now, I rejoice. My sometimes conflicting layers coupled with my health challenges often make the concept of dating and being courted unappealing, but at times it grows on me -briefly.

...

Before I know it, morning arrives. My eyes open rather reluctantly. *Thank you, Lord, for another chance.* I take inventory of today's symptoms after my time in the Word and prayer, then proceed to see if I can walk today. *Okay, so far so good.* I get up and go to the bathroom, throw water on my face, and brush my teeth. I head downstairs in search of my laptop. I'm determined to get some work done, but first my tea.

So floor we meet again... Alright, get up girl, just breathe. Crawling as an adult is some kind of experience. Your perception has since changed. You're heavier so it's harder to do. Randomly, I begin to think of how my life would look differently if I had a family like many of my contemporaries. Would I work and travel as much as I do? Would I be free like I am now? *Am I sincerely free or am I just downright detached?* These are not typically questions that keep me up at night, but after talking to my mom and with this ten-year reunion hanging over me, I can't help but think on these things. I can't say I'm unhappy, but I wouldn't say I'm happy either… I have happy moments -I guess. I'm not depressed or anything, but I'm straight. Of course I know that my joy comes from God and that is a constant. It is something that one has to learn to find even in the most trying of circumstances, but happiness is temporal. Sometimes happiness is a choice, but it can still be fleeting nonetheless.

While I'm still on the floor desperately trying to get out of this stupor, I am transported back in time to an event put on by my first business baby, Dope. The subject of mental health in the Black community came up, and I am very much a proponent of people utilizing all the resources available. Mental health is health, but at that moment, I remember questioning my integrity because I accused myself of being a fraud. I was technically diagnosed with depression years ago a few months after I was diagnosed with a disease from the land of make-believe that somehow made it out of Storybrooke. My primary care physician at the time essentially asked me if I wanted to address it and of course I declined. I simply replied, "No" when she inquired, "Do you think you're depressed?" Maybe I lied. Maybe I didn't. *I didn't think I was or maybe only a little, but if a fake disease turned your life upside down during a time some call the best years, you probably wouldn't be too happy either.* Well, I suppose it doesn't really matter in the grand scheme of things. I'm making it the best I can. *That could be up for debate but whatevs.* In retrospect, I probably was just having a bad day and my emotions matched how I felt physically. Depression is very real and should be addressed, but as humans we have emotions -even folks like me who aren't always in tune with them. Being sad, upset, uneasy is normal when you get knocked off your square. Sometimes you get tired of fighting, especially when it's your own body. Some days you just wake up and yell "AGAIN, WE HERE AGAIN!!!!" at the top of your lungs, then you shake it off 'cause it could be worse, 'cause sometimes life isn't just rainbows and sunshine and you learn that coping is important. I'm accepting that it is okay for me to acknowledge I'm having a bad day without it just being complaining or people viewing it as a lack of faith. God is good, but I don't have to pretend I feel good when I praise anyhow, and having a bad day isn't the same as being chronically or clinically depressed. I didn't allow them to speak that over my life at the time.

Surprise

November 1, 2021

This morning is a little better than yesterday, so I'm grateful. I decided to work for a few hours, but I put myself on a schedule in hopes that the alleged workaholic tendencies don't set me back. As I stroll down the hall to my home office, I decide to open up all the blinds. I usually keep it dark here, but today I need more light. I contact my managers and get up to speed on what's happening at HQ and respond to pressing emails. I really want to get back to the café today, but knowing me I'll push it, so that's tomorrow's goal. In the meantime, I have Sam video conference me so I can see my kitchen. By 2pm I stick to my schedule and relax. I'm learning that resting outside of bedrest is not laziness. In fact, it's necessary. After working, I review Sunday school and children's church materials. Before I know it, I tap out, grab snacks, and get cozy in my favorite spot to watch Christmas classics.

As I am winding down, my phone goes off and I am frozen in time once I read the name of the sender. He's the infamous 'him' of my adolescence. I came to call him "Grey," which wasn't an arbitrary name. The day we met at the beginning of 11th grade, he deemed me his soulmate, but I didn't think much of it at the time. After having my grades frozen and leaving school early due to tremors, he and Gina were really the only people from school I spoke to. He technically was my high school boyfriend. He and I had a complicated friendship, truthfully a situationship on and off for about six years. I must say, I did learn a lot from my experiences with him, good and bad. One of the most profound nuggets I uncovered is that some things are better left in the past. I haven't told anyone that we ran into each other a couple days ago, it was definitely awkward.

I was still feeling like crap, but okay enough to fake it. I went out for a drive and to a little meeting a bit on the personal side. I was walking out of my meeting concentrating on not looking ill while scolding myself for being out in the first place. I was minding my business, *which I'm really good at,* when I spotted him. I was not having it. *Talk about petty...* He was with an adorable little boy who I knew was his son. In that instance, I was transported back in time, but I had to think fast before the current fully swept me away. My goofy behind tried to hide in the doggon bushes! LIKE FA REAL I WAS IN THE BUSHES! Black people don't do that kinda stuff or at least not my Black people... I have never, not-a-nan time, in over a decade knowing this dude ran into him, but then there he was. Of course, this negro spiritual saw me AND unlike a decent human being, he did not ignore me and pretend like he didn't see me attempting to hide in the bushes! *Me and them bushes woulda been just friggin fine.* Grey approached the bushes and looked down at me with a smug smirk on his face while I was looking' stupid. I was in the dirt in vain. I just wanted to go home and take a shower and forget that ever happened.

I faked a smile and stifled the laugh of knowing full well I was mortified. "Oh, heeeyyyyyy. I umm I umm dropped something in the bushes, but I found it so yayyy," I said. *Yeah, I found my face on the ground.*

He was still smiling, and I knew that nigga was laughin' at me. I could only hope my face wasn't showing the words I wanted to say. I silently prayed to the Lord to please get me out of there!

"And who is this handsome fella you got with you? Is this Junior?" I asked.

"Yes, he is, say hi to Ms. K," he replied.

My phone went off, and before I knew it, I said "Oh thank God! You are real!" I felt him looking at me like an idiot, so I went on to say "I've been waiting on this call for like a week. Ya know? Business stuff and all that. So umm it was gr- good to see you. It's been a while. Maybe we'll talk soon." In a softer tone, I looked at the little boy and said, "Bye sweetie."

"We will," he said. *Boy please.* I got the heck up out of there and answered the phone as quickly as possible for it to be a wrong number.

On the ride home, I was transported to the day that Grey told me his baby was on the way. I was devastated. Just a few months prior to this news, he painted a picture of the beautiful family which was to one day be ours, but it was still *if*. It's funny because, in retrospect, it was always this alternate universe because we weren't realistically compatible. Keisha used to tell me she would have never put us together, but somehow, we worked at the time. Truthfully, I think we should have just been unlikely friends or even left it at acquaintances, but there is no time for regrets.

My freshman year in college was when my health kept taking turns and the flare ups became too fierce for me to live in my dorm. When I moved back home and began to commute, I was alone outside of my family. Most of my friends were on campus or out of state. I remember sitting in his room doing homework while he played video games. I remember the nights of us sitting in the car talking about life for hours. I recall when I was scared and ashamed of being scared and feeling weak or actually feeling at all and was only comfortable telling him. I remember telling him I was sick because I knew he wouldn't care and wouldn't treat me like an invalid. We had a semblance of a friendship, and he was the only boy I ever fell in love with. We never put any effort into anything real. We were kids growing into adulthood, *according to him I was already grown*. We had wildly different plans and foundations. I won't make it seem like he was an awful individual, and I won't lie like I didn't truly love him because I did and probably always will have love for him in some way, but I rejoiced when I stopped being in love with the version of him I created in my mind back then. I learned a lot, and learning can never be a loss. I guess this ten-year reunion has me getting a little nostalgic. *Ion like dat.*

Grey sent me a congratulatory text about the show. Whenever we'd come back in contact, that's normally how. He was the first person to congratulate me when I preached my first sermon. He was genuine in it, though he doesn't even believe in the Gospel. We respected each other's polar opposite views and shared commonality in other areas, often cultural. I am happy to hear he's doing well, and it was surreal to see him as a dad in living color.

...

I wake up determined to shake off the thoughts of the past. As I place my glasses on my face and get into my morning rituals, I look forward to having a house full soon. Tomorrow is the watch party!

Everyone will be here: my parents, CoCo, Danielle, my close friends, my part-time kids, e'rybody. It'll be one of those parties you hear about in a Luther song. But tonight is girls' night out to celebrate the show, so I will myself to be well enough to wear a pair of my favorite stilettos and wear a dress that makes people wonder "that's what preachers look like" while still being unable to call it racy. It's my best friend Brittany's turn to drive and it's still beyond me that she has a minivan. She wanted that before my God babies came. *Out here tryna be somebody's daughter and Nurse Brit got us in a minivan. It betta be some snacks in this mug.* Tonight entails supporting the competition for some uppity eats and taking in some culture. We supported some local artists. The gala I totally forgot I was supposed to go to was at a new art studio off Fashion Ave. We even got free drinks. No matter how far along you get financially, it's still nice to get free stuff. Ambitiously we head out to a lowkey lounge to kick it. I prefer places with a dance-if-you-want-sit-if-don't kind of vibe.

...

The excitement of today has pushed last night's fun times aside. Today I am Ana at the beginning of Frozen telling the guards to open up the gates. I'm so excited I can't stand myself. I have a freakin' cooking talk show! Somebody should pinch me so I know it's real. *Wait. Nope, nevamind. Them reflexes be hittin'.* After the party comes to an end, my mom, CoCo and I decide to have a little sleepover. Daddy left us and went to their house. When I built this house, I had a guest house or as I like to call it the mini house built on for my parents. They have this dope RV and love being semi-retired snowbirds. They have projects going too and they consult for me. We keep it all in the family. They have a property in Phoenix and kept the family house, but every now and then they stay here.

Once my sister is out for the count, Mommy and I end up talking as we always do when we're trying to go to sleep. I ended up telling her about my personal meeting I hadn't gotten around to telling anyone about.

"Momma, I think it's time."

"Time for what?" She asks.

"To jig!" *Aahaaaaaa! I crack myself up sometimes.*

She tries to stifle her laugh to not wake CoCo and says, "You so goofy! Whose child are you?"

"Yours girlfriend, but okay seriously Momma. I think it's time…"

Something New, Something Old

"Mommy, it's time to adopt. I wanna go find my daughter. I've been praying. You've known I wanted to do this for years and I had a meeting with a social worker from the adoption agency a few days ago."

"I know how you get when your mind is made up, but are you sure?" she asks concerningly.

"Yes, Momma. And now you and Daddy will finally be grandparents, for real now."

"Well, honey. I am behind you 100% I just want you to know what you're getting yourself into…"

"I do, well I'm learning. The social worker is beginning the process and doing all my preliminary background checks and much to my advantage you and Daddy raised some good kids. My only concern is that they will consider my health unlike the laxed and extremely unprofessional vetting of that CPS worker before. They don't just give babies to anyone, well sometimes I think they do."

I've been through a similar process getting custody of Ivy, but I'd like to think I'm more equipped this time around. Plus, I'm starting

before the teenage years, and I imagine the
probing I'll endure this time will not just be
utterly pointless invasions of privacy and total
disregard for my time. Dealing with some of the
CPS and Foster Care workers was hell for more
than just me.

*Well, I guess I should at least try to sleep. I have to
be at the set earlier than I'd like.* Going to set is
one of the very few reasons I schedule my day to
begin before ten or so in the morning. I never
know how my body is going to cooperate. Here's
hoping…

…

Being awake and being up are two completely
different things. I always learned that the hard
way when I worked night shifts occasionally
through college. I always preferred coming home
at this time than leaving. I rush to get ready and
head out the door being careful not to wake
anyone.
Coastin' down the freeway, I fall into my music
and try to get my mind right. As I get closer to set,
I say a little prayer to prepare myself. I still get
nervous in front of cameras. Today's show should
be fun. It's the end of October, so we are talking
about tradition and whatnot with Negro Spiritual
and Indigenous Gathering Day being right around

the corner. Other people would call it
Thanksgiving but whatever.

"3, 2, 1…"
After my introduction, the words just flow: "Soul
food is cleaning greens, cutting them, and mixing
my spices while waiting to put them in the pot
with smoked meat and every element coming
together to make a sweet symphony. Soul food is
filling the house with aroma, hearing people
fussin' while trying to listen to Luther Vandross.
Soul food is remembering how it felt when I made
my first cake from scratch. Soul food is when my
great aunt asks for my recipes and when my
friends equate my yeast rolls to that of the caliber
of their grandmothers. It is my friend proclaiming
that if I cook, she'll eat. Soul food is how I live my
life. Soul food is but a dream which is played out
when I get to step into the kitchen. Well folks, if
you guessed what's on the menu you would be
correct. If I have never before made food for the
soul, I surely shall today."

While I was making the greens, I couldn't help but
think about my first rheumatologist. He was a
fairly nice old white man, I suppose. During one
of my follow-ups it came up that I like to cook and
that I am the greens-maker in my family. He
asked me about the process, so I told him, and he
was so enthralled and astounded. It was flippin'

hilarious. This man looked me in my optimal stems trying to gauge an understanding of this Black staple, and he asked, "What would it be if you didn't add the greens?" Trying not to laugh, I responded, "Like a meat broth or potliquor..." Then this man said what has burned into my brain forever, "So it's like a warm salad!" That is still funny. The audience thought it was a hoot.

This episode was everything! After years, I finally perfected my ode to my Granddaddy, which is my sweet potato pie that has a special ingredient that takes most by surprise. I don't fully remember how it tasted, but I know it was delicious, especially with whipped cream. So, of course we made fresh whipped cream. As an added treat, I featured my sweet potato pie cupcakes inspired by my cousin, the baking sensation in Montgomery. They start with a layer of that pie filling, vanilla cake, then frosted with a cinnamon citrus buttercream, and sprinkled with streusel. It's one of my favorite things to make. I had worked on this recipe for years trying to get it right; though I know it's different from my Granddaddy's, it still takes me back to being at the old house. I share as much as possible without giving away too many family or trade secrets. Recipes Mama used and the recipes I cultivated just for my family don't even make it to the café. Some things should be held dear.

...

My Ride-Or-Die, Rave', is a journalist, producer, editor, and now actress. She was writing an article on holiday traditions some time ago before finishing one of her degrees not long before climbing the ladder in New York then Cali to become the big shot she is today. With us being brought up so proud of our Black culture, she asked me to expound on soul food and what it meant to me. She asked a few other people as well, but I can only speak on how the inquiry resonated with me. It astounds me how food can be so nostalgic. Food is such an avenue.

With this time of year approaching, my thoughts of Mama become more frequent. The first couple Christmases after her passing, we didn't make her original five cookies. A few years back CoCo, Danielle, and I decided that we didn't want the tradition to die so we started again, but it lacked a bit of the spirit without her yelling at us like we were elves and she was Sassy Country Claus. Now we take turns yelling. I think this year CoCo and Dani are coming over so we can make them here. I have to call them to make sure. Man, this time next year I may even have my own little elf, but I can't get too excited; adoption can take some time, and there are no guarantees.

After a few final reshoots and a bit of plotting on what we will do for the Christmas special, the whole day is just about gone, so I check my emails in my dressing room and I am so thankful that Michele is holdin' it down at the café. I leave very specific instructions for when I am not there, and I monitor as much as possible remotely without full on micromanaging. I try to find balance so my staff still feels free to exercise their gifts and skills while keeping in line with the mission and setup of my establishment. I also double check to make sure that leftover food at the end of the day doesn't go to waste but instead goes to food rescue missions. Apparently, I need to go have a nice chat with some staff at headquarters though… Every now and then newbies get a little beside themselves when they don't see the big boss enough, but I can rectify that. Upon leaving the studio, I make a long day even longer and head to headquarters for an impromptu visit because I got time today.

As I walk in, I see the shook looks on their faces. I'm not positive, but I am pretty sure that my face says it all. I call everyone into the conference room. I enjoy being the laid-back employer everyone comes to know and love, but I need for there to be no confusion. I endure enough chaos, so I will not have foolishness running amuck in my business. I literally paid all the costs to be the boss. *Like er'y single one of 'em.*

"Good afternoon everyone. I know some of the newer faces I have only briefly met while others have been here for a while and know how I run things. You can say I run a tight ship, but we have a familial, fun, and relaxed office culture here. I know I have a solid team, but I have heard that there was a bit of confusion. I love a free-flowing environment and despite my reputation and the name I do not press hierarchy much, but make no mistake I approve every hire and every check. I appreciate all ideas and credit is given where credit is due, I give incentives, and this corporation provides flexibility and so much more, but if you would like to run things your way, I reckon you leave and find a better fit. I value each and every one of you, and with that being said, disrespect will not be tolerated. If you cannot get with the purpose of this corporation and respect the position you hold, the door is there, and your resignation will not be disputed. Thank you for your time and service. Our office Christmas party is coming up soon. Details will be disbursed in about a week or so. Good day."

I'm not in the mood to entertain questions. I was not calling anyone out by name because they know who they are. I simply don't have the time, so I'll see what happens by Jesus' birthday celebration. There may be a few changes to come at the beginning of the year. Heading down to the café, I chat with a few of our regulars, talk to my manager Samantha about new orders, go over the upcoming chef's specials to come and plan for our upcoming themed nights. Finally getting home, it is past midnight.

Before I wind down, I need to see tomorrow's agenda because I refuse to have another long day after this one. I always said I wanted my weeks to look different and now most days look different too. Scrolling through tomorrow's obligations, I see I forgot about a meeting with a client. One of our largest contracts is with a project management firm based in Ohio. All the work happens in Michigan, but every now and then I have to go show my face to the company heads. Looks like I'll be going on a road trip tomorrow. Since my parents are still in town, I might as well have them tag along and we can see some family and stay over the weekend. Courty may come too. I think she'll still be here.

...

I always learn so much about my dad when we go on road trips, like how he dabbled in stand-up comedy during his army days, how my top-secret theory of him having been in the mafia could still be true, and how he remembers when he first saw my mom, so I guess now is as good of a time as any. I might as well share with CoCo today also. Sometimes she feels out of the loop being so far away.

"Daddy, I had a meeting with a social worker the other day."

"A social worker? For what?"

"About adoption."

"Adoption? Baby girl, are you sure?"

"Yes, Daddy. I want a little girl. I know I'm supposed to be somebody's mom." I rarely ever talk to my dad about my dating life, like ever, but I'm pretty sure this conversation is somehow going to go in that direction.

"You don't want to *have* kids?" I know that had to cut him to say that out loud. It takes my mom to talk with him when it comes to CoCo and me. He has a hard time seeing me as a grown woman. *Boy, this is going to get interesting.*

"Just because I'm adopting doesn't mean I don't want to give birth to children. I just know I have a kid out there who's mine. I would like to get married and have babies one day, but even in adopting she'll be my baby. She'll bear our family name. You'll be her granddaddy. And if possible, one day I'll give her siblings. She won't be a tester baby as if I'm using her to decide if I want a family of my own. She'll be my family whether the day comes for me to marry or not."

"Are you sure you can handle it?"

"Yes Daddy. I believe I can."

The awkward silence doesn't last very long as Phil Collins's "Live" album plays and I begin to crush it on the air drums and vocals for one of my all-time favorite songs, "In the Air Tonight." CoCo and Mommy are in their own bubble during our little conversation, but I'm sure my parents will reprise this amongst themselves soon. When we arrive, I have them drop me off at the client's headquarters and they go ahead to see our relatives.

...

After the negotiation of the renewed contract is done, I am now free to rejoin my family. It's always good to see everyone. It's a home away from home. Family, food, laughs, cards, music. This is us. *Oh crap! Just that fast. Something isn't right. My body is crashing in on itself, but I'm trying to hold it together and look normal.* I find an excuse to retreat and go lay down before anyone notices.

In the span of a few mere hours I went from dazzling, domineering business woman *okay maybe just business woman* preparing to adopt a baby to barely carrying myself to bed. This is really inopportune. This stays happening when I got something to prove. *Lord, send help. Please. It often feels like my body punishes me for living.*

Finally

Thankfully, we were able to still have a merry time, but our visit was short-lived. After a few hours in the car, we are back home in the city that I love. My mother, however, decides to circle back to this something-isn't-right guilt trip. I'm not feelin' the rigmarole. My parents always want to take extra precautions when I have really bad flare-ups or when something new or acute surfaces. I get it, but I just want to shower and get in my beautiful big bed.

I suppose one day soon I'll know the love and concern of a parent, prayerfully nothing like this scenario though... I wouldn't wish this kind of life on anyone, even though outside of being sick life is pretty smooth. I just hate the weight of knowing that I've added to their stress for so long. I know it's out of my control, but that doesn't make it any more palatable. Half the time I seek medical attention is for their reassurance, but frankly I'm tired of medical bills and I do not have the capacity to handle a medical professional saying something stupid to me today. I'm not anti-doctors or anything, but I've had some very unpleasant encounters from blatant racism, sheer incompetence, extreme condescension, pure negligence, and the list continues. Them not knowing is one thing, and even some of the misdiagnoses I could get past, but those issues I've experienced as a Black woman in America have been abominable, especially while I was younger. Now that I can heavily advocate for myself, I don't have time. I do pray not to be bitter and to listen to my body when I need to. This balancing act gets so off-balance at times.

> "Fine. I will make an appointment. Okay?!"
> "Watch your tone!" *My Mom is so not my best friend right now!*
> "Yes ma'am."

> ...

Gosh dang it! So, I'm kinda on the floor again. Hopefully nobody notices. Why oh why could my body not have yielded to me and just waited to act like a jerk until I got into the privacy of my bedroom?! Foolishness like this always happens when I'm tryna prove a point. Welp, I guess pride came before the fall, quite literally.

> *While still in a daze, I am transported back in time. I stared at the ceiling on the dining room floor at Granny's house. When Mommy was no longer zoned out and into her work, she heard my struggle and rushed out of her seat. At that moment, I could no longer take the rage and frustration that filled my body. I thought I*

*put away rage along with anger as the
Bible tells me, but it boiled high, so high in
that moment. Tears began to fall down my
face and hit the floor. I can still hear each
tear pitter pat on the hardwood.
"Mommy, I'm scared. They don't know
what's wrong with me and I'm so tired." I
normally tried to keep my fear to myself, to
reject it and not give it voice, but Mommy
knew... She knew even without the betrayal
of my once sonorous voice being shaky and
weak.
"I know, baby. We all are, but it's going to
be okay."*

I came to after a few seconds, but each one was a
second too long. Since I'm not as dependent on
my parents as I was not so long ago I don't ask for
permission. They can't just pick me up when I
have severe flare-ups, holding me hostage at
Granny's house because they don't want me to
fall down the stairs. I understand their reasoning
because I indeed have fallen down the stairs
when left alone during severe ones, but I need my
freedom. My sense of independence needed to be
restored. Well, really it needed to be formed. I
was not going to let my health dictate my entire
life. It's affected enough, and now I'm sure my
dad is going to try to change my mind about
adoption. I'm going to bed and they can't make

me go to the stupid doctors anyway. *I'm grown. I'm not going!*

...

So here I am at the stupid ER with my parents. CoCo is sitting in here waiting on the doctor to come in while I pray we don't catch any nasty germs up in here.

"You ever think you have too much going on?"

"Nope."

"Kenny."

"Courty."

"I'm serious," she says exasperatedly.

"Me too."

"I worry about you."

"I know, but you shouldn't. If we pray, we ought not to worry," I say matter-of-factly.

"I know, but Kenny you got a lot going on in your body and you do an awful lot. You've amassed so much before 30 and I want you to see 60 and 90 God-willing."

"Coco, as our movie 'Soul Men' teaches us 'At the first slap and cry we all start to die, but I ain't on no accelerated program!'"

"Can you be serious for one minute?!"

A heavy sigh escapes, "I know this is serious. Yes, it can make life suck at times, but God gave me too much to lay in bed every day and truthfully I'm not that sick where I have to be on a daily basis. I empathize with the sick and shut-in, but I will not be lumped in with them if I can help it. That is not my testimony, at least not right now, and I'm not going to let something unnamed win. I know there are days when I am bedridden. I know there are times when I am in the hospital, but I take care of myself. I take precautions, but I'm careful for nothing."

"I love you sister."

"I love you, too, now stop worrying and start getting excited to be an auntie."

"Mmmm you got something you want to tell me?" She looks at me quizzically.

"Don't have a coronary. I'm adopting. I already started working with an agency."

...

The hospital admitted me, but if I have to just wait this thing out, I can rest at home, not in this uncomfortable environment. *Okay Kenny, be intentional about not complaining!* On the other hand, I might actually get bugged less here. Reception is terrible so I can't even check on work very much. I guess it'll do for one night.

...

Upon being discharged, we head back home. When I am left alone for a moment, I send some emails and make a few calls to make sure everything is running smoothly at work, especially after the tension had been so thick at HQ. I also video chat with Michele and send CoCo to check on things for me in person. For the most part, she knows how I want things done and she trained a lot of my wait staff. I'll probably go in myself in two or three days since that's when I unveil next month's chef's menu. I typically kick off and end the new menus while my no limit soldiers hold it down during the in between time. *I have to get better. Body, act right.* I earnestly ask God to heal my body. My moment of alone time comes to an end as my parents enter my bedroom to check on me and hang out for a bit. They never really know what to do to make me feel better, but they do everything they can possibly think of to try. While this moment lasts and Mommy is once again my best friend, I suggest we have a 'Godfather' marathon.

...

It's now morning, and I'm not the only one up at the crack of dawn. CoCo went downstairs to begin preparing to go back to work before we all reunited for the holidays. When she went exploring in my kitchen, she stumbled upon one of my prized possessions. When I finally make it downstairs, I see her staring at it pleasantly surprised.

"I can't believe you still have this."

"Of course I do. It's my favorite apron. One, you got it for me for a birthday, two it has my name on it, and three it's denim and you know I love singing the word denim like ole dude in that old Target commercial."

Maybe I'm more sentimental than I thought.

After she's done packing, my parents take her to the airport. While they're out, I take in the freedom and my mind goes back to business. I check in with my team at headquarters and with my staff at the café. I can't wait to be back in my kitchen.

...

After a few days at home, I'm finally sprung. It's barely seven o'clock in the evening and I am spent. A five-minute call turned into thirty minutes, but that's not so bad; sometimes people just need someone to listen. It did take my little energy though, so I'm going to carry myself back to my bed.

Things are always so hectic before the holiday season, and it doesn't help that my body is still cussing me out. I must get better for the chef's menu debut tomorrow. *My business babies really be havin' me rippin' and runnin'. One start cryin' then all of 'em need somethin'. They might need a daddy for real, but I can't tell my Momma that.*

Before I prepare for bed, Mommy comes in and we have our daily chat. Normally her and Daddy aren't still in Michigan around this time. They are usually at their Phoenix property and we pick a place to go for Christmas, but of course they don't want to leave me here like this... After we wish our goodnights, I try desperately to sleep. No matter how long I keep my eyes shut, sweet restful sleep does not fall over me. I'm so restless. I toss and turn. I look into the abyss trying to keep my existential thoughts at bay hoping to give my overloaded mind a break.

...

As morning breaks, I'm still weak, but I'm going to push on to the café. I'm rushed off my feet, but the adrenaline keeps me high. I always love debuting special menus. Just before the dinner rush there's normally a lag so I get with Michele and the rest of the kitchen staff to discuss the holiday headliners. I just want to make sure we are prepared. We wrap up just in time for a flood of people, as expected for a Friday night. It is going to be a long night. It's a vibe tonight, but I'm having a hard time keeping up the pace, so I'll be leaving shortly. I take my time going home. The city seems calm like everything and everyone is at peace tonight. I know that ain't reality, but in my heart I wish it were. To finally be at peace is a blessing beyond words. Sometimes we think we have to pass away to get it, but "as it is on Earth as it is in Heaven..." I'm learning that being at peace does not mean everything is perfect in the societal definition, but God grants peace that surpasses all understanding and I think I'm getting to that gift. I feel so close to it, *sometimes.*

I'm trying to be intentional in my stride to be content in any and every circumstance. I want to be a wife someday, but I can find happiness before that happens, if it happens. I want kids, but I am okay right now even though I don't have them yet.

I'm trying to love myself and show myself grace, not make excuses to keep sinning when I fall or allow myself to wallow when I need to walk, but to truly give myself grace and accept what is out of my control trusting that I serve the One who is. On a weekly basis, I have to cast out doubt when it comes to my body wondering if it'll make it through whatever I have up that week, but I remember I can do all things through Christ who strengthens me. The purpose is bigger than me, so He has made provisions and contingencies. It still amazes me that He uses me, so I'm learning to love what He gave me. *Lord, You made wonders of this world. You created the entire galaxy, yet You still made me knowing I'd fail you, knowing good and well I'd be a mess. Thank You Lord for choosing to love me still.*

Aside from my fat girl complex from being a fat kid. I'm ascertaining how to love my body, not just embrace my curves and accept visible imperfections, but this body has been through a lot. I've hated what it's gone through and in turn often hated this body. So now I have to be intentional about looking in the mirror and being grateful. For my legs, because I know what it's like to hardly be able to walk and for them to give out, so I'm all the more grateful when they hold me up. For my stomach, because I know what it's like to be sick to my stomach sometimes for weeks straight or even more and I am grateful when I digest properly. For my arms, because they can carry so much even though they've been weak and hurting. For my back, because I know how immense pain can cause me to hunch over or not move at all, but with deliberate perfect posture it helps me strut tall with dignity. I am grateful for my hands, though they cramp up, because they make magic in the kitchen. Sickness can be humbling, but I finally see that hating what my body has been through led to self-loathing and that is not of the God I serve. That self-loathing at its root is insecurity. There's a thin line between humility and insecurity. The latter breeds sin; it can even mimic pride. The chronic ailments I face are not direct results of what I've done to myself, though I too experience cause and effect like everybody else, but bitterness is up to me. My reaction will only make me better or worse. I have to choose to be a good steward of this body because it's still here. I'm still here and there's more to this life than just work to do. Finally, I'm seeing.

Lord, help me to walk in humility even if that means breaking me. I may not like it, but Lord help me seek Your face in all things and glorify You.

Last night, my mind unexpectedly took me down Memory Lane. This morning, I am determined to cleanse my little mind and take inventory. Alright, I preach next week, so I need to prepare and consecrate myself for that. I meet with the social worker early in the morning, and I have dinner with Mommy and God-Mommy after I leave the café. I got a feeling those ladies are going to double team me. I haven't talked to Auntie Cookie in like forever, but I know Nita told her about this adoption. *Ah whatever, I'll cross that bridge when I get to it.*

Rosalind Ferrell was all in; today was the start of the grueling process. They requested background checks, medical records, and references. She will be scheduling interviews with my family and friends. She'll also be dropping by my house for both unexpected and planned visits. It's getting pretty real.

"Hey Mommy! Hey God-Mommy!"
"Hey there Kenny! You always look so nice it's a wonder you don't have a fiancé," says Auntie Cookie. *Here we go. She means well, but that's really not the compliment people think it is.*

"You just skipped boyfriend straight to fiancé!"says Nita. *At least Mommy noticed too! Sheesh!*

"Well thank you God-Mommy, but I look a mess. I came straight from the café. How have you been?"

"I've been really good..."

I'm sure Nita recruited her to reassure me how difficult it is being a single mom, and how dating will be even more challenging with a kid. Honestly, I don't even like dating like that. Trying to keep myself interested in someone new is trying. I'm either feelin' you or I'm not. Plus, I have a lot to think about when it comes to dating because I'm not a serial casual dater. When I date there's a purpose, not that I think every guy is potentially "theee guy," but if certain values and intentions aren't aligned, we might as well go on about our business.

After a long day, I sit and reflect on my conversation with Mom and Auntie Cookie, but it changes nothing. I know it won't be a cakewalk, but what is? I will have to screen them before these interviews though... *Momma been tellin' me I'ma make a good lil mommy since my adolescent years, but now that I wanna be a good lil mommy, everybody got a problem because it's not how they planned.*

Life does not always work out the way we plan. *God is probably laughing at the plans I call myself having right now.* Now I just go with it. I used to think about age and how I needed to reach certain milestones, but really time didn't matter. I mean time matters, but it does not have to be a measurement of success.

Speaking of time, my birthday is this month. I'm almost thirty… *Didn't I just say time didn't matter? Gosh I'm so conflicted.* On one hand, I've apparently accomplished a lot before thirty, but on the other hand I didn't expect it to look like this and I'm not where I want to be. That's the conundrum we humans seem to face when we are positioned between what one would call a rock and a hard place. Why are we never satisfied? *Why am I never satisfied? I thought I was pretty content in life, but I be trippin sometimes. I must learn the Apostle Paul's secret to being content in any circumstance.*
My phone rings and interrupts my thoughts. It's Mia's boyfriend. Aman called to confirm some details for her party. It's difficult surprising her, so of course he recruited the best person for the job if I do say so myself. I am catering this intimate gathering personally, and he's flying her parents in, and we're getting all of her close friends to come. I like him for her. It's high fashion themed because during college she modeled. It'll be fabulous. I have to tell her that I'm in Texas to meet with the entertainment law

firm to negotiate a contract for Black Out. I do actually have to do that, so I need to add prepping for that for me to-do. The majority partner emailed me last week to schedule. Hopefully, this timeline works as well as it does in my head.

After ending my call with Aman, I'm grateful for the reminder. Once I square away details for this party, I check in with the team and go over a few things with Meaghan, Haley, and Michele. I also need to set up interviews to get a new assistant. Haley stayed on a bit longer since she still has time before she officially needs to be in South Carolina. I'm bringing in chocolate mousse cake as a well wish and thank you. She is so brilliant and incredibly sweet. I'm still sending her a bonus for Jesus' birthday. I think I'll hire someone after the first of the year, so I won't worry about interviews today. Even though this can be one of our busiest times of year, it'll add too much stress finding someone to help with the load so close to deadlines. Thankfully most of the operation will be closed for a bit soon. Really, the only fully operational entity will be Kenny's Kitchen and it has special hours for the holidays. I don't want to miss money, but I have to prioritize my people before profit. I walk the line of caring for my employees and meeting demand. I wouldn't be able to do what I do on the scale I do it without them.

There's so much happening this month. I'm tired already. I keep telling myself I'm going to take a real vacation for my birthday or have a party or something. To this day, I've never been on a real vacation. Family trips are great, work trips have been cool, and I love visiting the homies in their respective cities, but a real vacation do-what-I-want, live-it-up kind of trip I have not had. Quick weekend getaways have been fun, but I've found a way to work on every single one or the elephant in the room starts making that trumpeting sound. I've often been ill on my birthday, and I received the first Storybrooke diagnosis just before my eighteenth birthday. I can hear Dr. Warm Salad saying, "There is no cure. There's no cure. There is no cure." With my mother to the right of me, all I did was stare at him. *I'm glad the doctors don't have the last say...* He went on to say, "You're just giving me a blank stare, what's happening here?" Was I supposed to cry or something? I suppose that would have been a natural reaction. Not to say that all birthdays have sucked; I'm always grateful for another year, but I haven't had one for the books, like a beautiful 'baecation', epic girls' trip, or just a marvelous unforgettable day. It hasn't happened yet. *I suppose I can make it happen. Not giving very much out of funds anymore should help, too.*

...

As morning dawns, an uneasiness sweeps over me. I think I had a bad dream last night while I was actually sleeping, but I can't fully make out what it was. In my morning prayer, I ask God to guide me and protect me. I find myself singing old Hymns this morning to overcome what's trying to come over me. It's probably fear stemming from yesterday's intervention or maybe it's even self-doubt, but either way it has to go. I continue to pray and speak life as I ready myself for the day.

Shaking off that unnerving sentiment, I start packing for my trip to Texas. In multi-tasking fashion, I have a conference call to make certain everything I need to handle is taken care of before I head out. I'm getting kind of excited for this trip. It's semi work, but it'll be a nice quick mental break. Maybe I'll go to that nice steakhouse Daddy and I found in El Paso. My stomach perked up just at the thought.

...

Oh the joys of traveling. I am T for tired, but I have to work a miracle. I need to close this deal to secure a contract for Black Out with the mucks of this law firm and pull together the dopest surprise party Mia Gina Akens has ever seen. Even though we mainly do consulting or administration, event coordination was actually what I wanted to do, but the problem was that everyone wanted to do it too. Because of that, I worked my strengths and event planning falls under management, so I get my fix from time to time through planning for the other entities and personal gatherings. I have a feeling I'll be planning a wedding soon. Aman is really serious about Mia and she's happy; they appear to thrive together, and I can see growth, which is substantial. She always used to laugh and think about a "That So Raven" episode when we were kids where Raven was running around as so many different people like a maniac because that'll apparently be me when she gets married. I'm allegedly helping plan the wedding, being the maid of honor, catering, and officiating the ceremony. I got this. I'll have to go into training, but I got this.

I was able to rent out this gorgeous contemporary style house with a fabulous kitchen. There's a massive pool and patio that accommodates a mock runway, each room on the main level had a different designer as a theme. The hardest part of this was finding her dress. For the most part I know her style and her size, but she is so particular. It's her favorite color, orange and I believe it is close to if not her favorite shade. This dress is so dang beautiful I got a goosebump! I think she'll love it! I hope she will.

...

I'm grinning all the way home because Mia's party was a huge success and I closed the deal with them Texan big shots who gone put Black Out, better yet, Braxton Holdings Inc. on the map! *Poppin, poppin, poppin!* Thank you sweet baby Jesus! *Out here givin' me gifts fa Your birthday.* I'm going to wash off this flight and then partake in Taco Tuesday 'cause I deserve it!

As I walk into one of my favorite spots in Southwest Detroit, I make eye contact with someone and I'm not immediately uncomfortable with awkwardly locking eyes with this complete stranger. He's sitting down but it looks like he's about 6'1. His deep, velvety chocolate skin is so clear. From here I don't see a ring or a tan line, but these days that may not mean much. *Who am I Fran Fine? Next thing you know I'll be able to tell you his occupation without even a hello.* I leave my glance at that and don't think anything else of this mystery man 'cause I'm taking in the authenticity of the culture and food of this joint and reveling in knowing that they use clean ingredients. I decide to eat my guilt-free comfort food and sip my sip there before returning to my sanctuary.

It's been a great couple of weeks. With so much excitement, I decided to chill this weekend not only because exhaustion is real, but it's so rare for me to plan to do nothing. The novelty of it makes it that much more worth it, though I do have one meeting to go to with a potential client. The café is under control. The new menu is working out great and Chels is a rock star. I need to start checking in on Dope more often though; that was my first baby and I have been neglecting her. As of late, I only go to our main events, the annual conferences and seminars. I also check in on our mentoring programs from time to time, but the apparel is typically approved electronically and I have as-needed meetings with the store manager. I have to do something for Akilah. She's been with me the longest and was my first full-timer. I think I'll wait until the season passes since I promised I'd relax this weekend before the Christmas traditions will be in full effect. Let me write myself a note and get ready for this meeting. I can't believe I scheduled a meeting on Saturday. I hope this goes well because I could surely be in a onesie, eating snacks, and binge watching all the new Black Christmas movies.

I think I'll ride the classic today, there's nothing like a Lincoln town car. I find myself reminiscing on driving my dad's blue '89 Lincoln town car. That boy stayed clean. Driving down our street, people would wave thinking they'd see a handsome, big, Black man, only to see me. Man, those were some good times, back when I wasn't responsible for the upkeep and still enjoyed all the benefits.

As I'm coasting through my neighborhood, I decide to take the scenic route. I turn on the radio and it's some rapper, if this even counts as rap; he's mumble-singing. It is a shame that music made over two decades ago was more futuristic than this. I hope he's not a Detroit rapper. I really try to support local artists, but somebody has to be the one to say "You know what baby boo...this ain't yo gift" or "Just stop it. Stop makin' a fool of yourself!" Thank God Leela James is going to make soul music until she can't anymore!

When I pull up to this fancy private office, I pray this is productive and efficient on time. *I got a date with my couch, so let's make this quick.* As I walked in the joint, there was no receptionist, but there's a familiar face, rather familiar eyes. *This is that beautiful specimen of a man I saw in Southwest Detroit last week. Is this a setup? This nigga might be a stalker. I think we're alone up in here. Oh hell naw! Good thing I stay ready... Pow Pow Pew Pew! Dang, he fine. I ain't realize how beautiful this man was. Is he the next potential Mr. Braxton? Focus nigga! Time to assess this situation.*

"Mrs. Braxton?"

"Mrs. Braxton is my mother. Just Miss, preferably Ms." *I see what you're doing here, buddy.*

"Hi Miss Braxton, I'm James Lucas."

"Nice to meet you. Shall we get started?" As a young, Black woman in business, I've had to learn how to play ball with the boys.

The meeting lasted about thirty minutes. He's an attorney and apparently a dang good one at that. This firm is a hidden gem with an impeccable reputation. I haven't really paid much attention, but Black Out deals a lot with law firms- approximately 50% of our clientele stem from law offices. It takes me back to my roots. My very first contract was with a very reputable criminal defense attorney. He laid out some of his needs and I explained what roles we typically play. We are supposed to reconvene Monday morning. I'm pretty sure we have this one in the bag, *but what I won't be is thirsty.*

Finally, I get home and before I can get too cozy, Joyce drops off my handsome nephew, Kelsey. *Welp, so much for that hot date.* I totally forgot I said I'd take Kelsey tonight. Kelsey is the sweetest though, so I don't mind. Kelsey's little brother, Ken, is with their Nana, so he's feeling special tonight getting me all to himself. Sometimes I miss when he was small and just watching cartoons sufficed, now I have to find games and keep his mind stimulated. Thankfully, this baby doesn't fight sleep. I will soon tuck my big boy in bed. He loves the car themed guest room. He calls it his room and sometimes throws in Ken.

Light is forced into my eyes as they are being pulled open by little hands, the beautiful aroma of bacon being fried fills my nostrils, and the sound of a soft voice singing "Happy Birthday, Auntie" awakens me. *Ima let it go that it's mad early because he's cute but this won't last.* My parents let themselves in this morning while I was still sleeping. Daddy is making breakfast. Mommy is making mimosas. Kelsey is reading me the card he made for me. *Life is good.* I still can't get over how big he is now. You'd think he really was mine. *This morning I can't help but think what it would be like if I was waking up to a baby of my own.* We missed Sunday School, but we made it to the main event. Kelsey is all hyped up because we're going to the mall and then go-kart racing after service. Since Ken came along, I make it a point to show both of them special attention making sure no one feels less loved than the other, so they both get their separate days and random gifts. When they really, really want to stay together I oblige and get them both. If I'm honest, they have me wrapped around their fingers.

...

Well the kid is happy, full, and worn out! And so am I and my wallet. We are done for the day! When we get home, Joyce pulls up shortly after. We chat and she hands me a gift. When I open it, my eyes nearly begin to leak. It's a personalized frame with pictures of my handsome boys and me. *I'm happy she's accepted she had them kids for me.* Being their Auntie brings me so much joy. It's truly a blessing that she supports our bond. *If I never get upgraded to Mom, I'll always be an Auntie.* After we have a brief adult girl talk session, they head out to get ready for the week.

As I walk them out, I stroll around my house as it is still so surreal. I was amazed at buying a house a couple years ago and fixing it up, bringing the kitchen up to code; but being able to build my dream home so soon truly gets me. I mainly use my first house for business purposes these days and for my family dinners for mentees. As I come up to the front door that I rarely use, I notice a package discreetly placed on my porch. It was either delivered when I was at the meeting yesterday or someone personally delivered it today. It's an engraved mortar and pestle, it's marble and it is absolutely gorgeous. It has my name on it! *I love my name on stuff! Okay, I admit. I may have a problem.* There's a card but no name on it. It reads "Happy Birthday! With love." Ashamed of where my thoughts were heading, I quickly stopped to find the perfect spot in my kitchen to place it.

When my parents come into the main house, they bring me gifts and food. My dad got me new mats for my Lincoln and Mommy got me some shoes from their trip to Italy. Why God chose to give me them I will never know, but I'll be forever grateful. Godmommy and her grandbabies Jayla and Jacob are right on time for dinner. Danielle even came through. When we cut the cake, something just feels right. I haven't made one of these in forever. It's a Chocolate Cognac Cake, *Hennessy of course they don't call me Kendawg with the Henndawg fa nothin,* filled with a fluffy white chocolate mousse and frosted in a chocolate Swiss meringue buttercream, adorned with a few chocolate shavings. *Thank me so much!* CoCo video called us to be a part of our

Negro Spiritual, too. What a beautiful way to end the night…

…

Alright Lord, what are we doing today? I have a meeting with Mr. Fine-Fa-No-Reason, Esq. then I'm off to the café. Because of the first task, I decided to be even more intentional on my attire today. I'm thinking of a slimming black midi dress with quarter length sleeves that complements my frame and one of my favorite pairs of shoes, black and red stiletto booties. I even put on a face. I'm happy this wasn't an early meeting, because adding makeup application to my morning routine was a bit of extra time. *I'm an 'if I'm ugly, I'm ugly, take me as I am" kinda chick. A lil fugly neva hurt anyone.*

> "Hi, I'm Braxton here for an 11 o'clock meeting with Mr.-" Before I can finish talking to the receptionist, Mr. Man rolls up.
>
> "Ms. Braxton. You're very timely. Nice to see you."
>
> "Yes, yes I am. Likewise, Mr. Lucas." *Well, today I'm timely…*

Once we shake hands, we walk down the hall and up a few stairs. He ushers me into his office that has a small conference table. This office is a cross between an art gallery and a contemporary home converted into an office. I would have never guessed that it was a law firm. Once we sit down, the deal is done. His needs are pretty parallel to much of our clientele. His firm will be outsourcing much of his firm's management needs. Black Out will be handling the larger projects, including coordinating all of the firm's engagements, conducting in-service presentations, providing basic training for his day-to-day administrative team, etc. He's drawing up the contract, which is novel because normally I do that. He doesn't know I'm technically a lawyer. I just don't practice law in the conventional sense. I went to law school and passed the bar, but I got it to make myself more knowledgeable and marketable in business. I own a corporation which owns businesses and invests in others, so it does come in handy. Plus I get to be a resource to my church home and community. My concentration was corporate law, however, I paid attention in the criminal courses. I knew I wanted to dabble in it enough so I could give free advice to some folks within my community, but I rarely find myself in the position to do so. That MBA/JD dual degree definitely paid off as a good investment. Black Out is not a law firm but keeping up with the Bar Association allows me to legally give advice and draw up contracts for my clients. Adding abbreviated legal services has been quite lucrative and I don't even charge what I could.

After we went through the contract, he was surprised at how quickly I signed. He looked at me quizzically and asked, "Don't you want your attorney to look at this?" I could not even try to stifle my amusement. I looked at him deadpan and said, "She did. I am my attorney," and placed the pen on the table and scooted my chair back to stand. *I picked the perfect pair of shoes for this moment.* Still with a puzzled look on his face, he gets up to walk me to the door. *Yeah nigga, I got degrees too, boo!*

I thought he was going to stop at the door, but instead he walked me to my car, *today was a classic Lincoln kind of day. Shut up, I'm the Lincoln Lawyer!* He was so composed before his mouth dropped, and now he has this smirk. I can't even find the words to describe it. I wouldn't call it smug, but it's surely not timid.

"The Mexican joint off Vernor Hwy... That's where I know you from, right?"

"I thought you just had a familiar face." *I mean he doesn't know me. He just saw me and maybe I remembered, but he ain't gotta know that.*

"Yeah, well now that our deal is signed on the dotted line, maybe I can take you out to dinner to commemorate this new partnership."

"The sentiment is very nice, but I don't make it a habit to fraternize with clients."

"Well this would not be personal technically. It's a business dinner or lunch, the first of many."

"Well I'll have to take a raincheck, Mr. Lucas, but only for legitimate business matters. Now, if you'll excuse me, duty calls."

"Have a nice day, Esquire." I say with the faintest smirk trying not to break out in awkward laughter. *Even in my head I laugh with my tongue out. I'm so ghetto.*

"Likewise."

Still Ti'ed

Every now and then, I try to be that chick who takes hot baths with candles and have my humidifier going with essential oils for aromatherapy to help me relax after a long day. Today would constitute one of those days. There's something mesmerizing about cascading water to me. My mind opens and my raspy voice runs freely. *I ramble even in my own thoughts.* As I turn the water off, I go into my nightly prayer and reflection. It has been the longest day I've had in a while, and I am tired, at least tomorrow is Hump Day. I feel like Wednesdays are more exciting when you don't control the whole operation, it's not like I'm closer to a day off or this concept of all play on the weekend. Between business and ministry, I very seldom have days off-let alone multiple in a row.

As morning dawns, I am awoken by my own exhaustion. *That's so backwards. I feel like a baby fighting her sleep, but instead I really want sleep, so what's fighting?* No need to rack my brain. I decided to stay in this cozy spot until about 9am. I want to relish this moment in the beauty of my bed. By the time I sluggishly get through my morning rituals, I opt to do conference calls instead of stopping in at headquarters and the Black Out office. As long as everything is running smoothly, or smoothly enough, I need not run myself too ragged today. I send memos to everyone I need to speak with and allow them to gather all my requested reports and settle into the respective offices at the complex.

I restored an old warehouse and made it into the home of Braxton Holdings Inc, including Kenny's Kitchen. I did that so it would be more convenient for me to maneuver through all entities whenever I needed, but it seems that lately I've been neglecting Dope and only going into Black Out when necessary. I guess that's how the seasons ebb and flow. Some seasons require me to give more attention to one and not the others. Everyone probably sees each other more than I see them. *Is this how parenthood will be if I have more than one?* I also allow flexible scheduling, so every office is not always open at the same time. The traditional 9am-5pm set up works for some people, but I was intentional about prioritizing the well-being of my employees. I believe in balance. My subconscious rolls her eyes at me like I'm lyin'. *Iight, iight fine. I believe in balance for my people. What can I say? I'm a work in progress.* As long as work gets done efficiently and my consumers' needs are met well, I'm good. Some days I'm so caught up in the Kitchen that I don't make it upstairs to address anything else. That could be a good thing though, the separation so to speak helps keep me focused on whatever the objectives are for that day. For this to be a one-stop-shop for everyone else, it doesn't seem to have the same effect for me most of the time.

While I wait for everyone to prepare themselves for the briefing, I go to the kitchen. I put on the kettle to make my tea. *I just love my baby Groot mesh tea ball. It makes making loose-leaf tea so much easier and baby Groot brightens up any day.* Once I take in my tea and get my act together, I go to my other house to begin to prep spice blends, house sauces and dressings that aren't made-to-order for the café, since this kitchen is still up to code.

Even though I can have someone else do it, I love spice hunting. When I go out to maintain my expansive collection, I get what's needed for the café, especially what's needed for the chef's menu since what's new is typically special order. I use the Ram to transport what can be prepped ahead of time when I know I'll be at home more than at the café such as today. Last night, I had the closing crew help me pack up and I let Michele go home early. Chels is so sweet. She's always here to do prep or anything I need her to, but everybody needs a break every now and then. Decompression is in every stir. I miss doing this sometimes, since most days I'm all over the place. *Be mindful of what you pray for 'cause you just might get it...* Before I know it, I'm lost in the sauce, and it's time to go be the CEO. I would take off this apron, but I'm just not invested enough. It's not like I'm addressing clients.

Praise God! Today's meetings weren't so tedious. My little chat with the associates at headquarters at the end of last month must have resonated. As I wrap up that little business, I go and pack up the truck and let the music guide me all the way to the Kitchen. When I pull up, the lunch rush is ending, giving me enough time to unload and review inventory before the dinner crowd steadily flows in giving us a run for our money.

Out of nowhere, Chele and Sam call me in the back as if there was some kind of emergency. When I rush to the back, thankful my clumsy self didn't trip over anything in front of everybody, I see balloons and a huge card that just about everyone signed. Meaghan, Haley, Akilah, and even Piper- the newest member of the family is here. They brought out a sheet cake and sang me happy birthday along with nearly everyone in the house. They even ordered me some pralines and chocolates from this candy shop I visit when I go to Myrtle Beach. They know I'm an intermittent sugar fiend. And it's not over, they, along with some of my go-to guys at Black Out, chipped in and got me a painting depicting all entities of the corporation with figures behind me representing them and their names are watermarked on it. Painted me is cute! *She poppin!* The painting captures everything! It even has my parents and sister on it, since all of my main people have worked with them in some way. They waited three days to do this so it would truly blindside me. *I actually like late birthday gifts, but they raggedy fa tryna get my eyes to drizzle.*

> "Y'all got me this time! Thank you so much! This is so sweet. I can't wait to hang this up in my living room! I have no words"

> "That's a first. Your hard work is an inspiration to all of us standing here and more. You go out of your way to make us feel more like family than employees and we wanted to give you a small token of our appreciation." Sam is holding back tears as she speaks.

> "I know I speak for us all when I say that we love you Kenny." *Not you too, Chels!*

> "Y'all lil heifas not gone have me goin' soft in here, at least not while customers are present. If we have a group hug, are the levees gone break?"

Before I know it, they bombard me. I'm in a full embrace. I never really noticed how many days I go without giving or receiving physical affection. Not that I'm a mean-hearted person, *I mean I know I'm kinda mean or at least perceived as such,* but I'm not what Nita calls "warm and fuzzy" according to most people's standards. Speaking of her, she's the only person I'm ever up under really. Maybe that's why I've been off, I haven't talked to my mommy since early yesterday morning when her and Daddy left for Cleveland.

As I come back to the present work at hand, I jump back into the groove after embracing the sentiment of their surprise. The hype dials back down some and the environment is like that of a movie scene. It's relaxing, yet vibrant. I love this place. When I look up, I nearly combust. *What the hell?*

"So Ms. Braxton, it's your birthday?" *Lord Jesus, is this man stalkin' me?*

"It was Sunday. They wanted to surprise me."

"Wait, you took meetings the day before and after your birthday? Now I really have to take you to dinner."

"That wouldn't constitute as a legitimate business encounter, now would it Counselor? And are you stalkin' me or somethin'?"

"Not at all. I just do my research and I appreciate good food. I also enjoy supporting black-owned businesses. And technically no, it wouldn't be business, but it would be a good time." *Dang this nigga charmin'*

"Are you flirting with me Mr. Lucas?"

"If you'll let me, yes. If not, then I used to be better at this," he says with a subtle yet suave facial expression.

"I told you I don't make it a point to fraternize with clients"

"Well, as this is your establishment and it is a sister to Black Out, of which I am a client, my meeting you here is something like a business encounter."

"The smirk on your face tells me that you know that's a big stretch sir."

"I do, but it was worth a try. Can I at least be a patron?"

"Well we don't turn down honest business. So please help yourself."

"Thank you, and happy birthday Miss Braxton." *Oh, so you gone hit me with the "Miss" this time, huh? I see.*

"Thank you so much. Enjoy the rest of your evening."

As I walk away, I try not to feel my oats too tough. I got an inkling that man is going to try me. *He gone try to wear me down and ain't nobody got time for that. He might mess around and start diggin' on me then I'ma think I'm feelin' him, but my emotionally guarded self gone realize that I'm not. Then he'll be hurt, but try to be too macho to say it and then before you know it I lose business. He might as well stop while he's ahead. Lord, why you make him so fine doe?* When I step back into the kitchen and those swinging doors sway behind me, I see the speculative looks these hussies have on their faces. They all collectively say "ooooh Miss Braxton."

"Fired! All of you!"

"So who was that Missssssssssssss Braxton?" I see Sam is the ringleader today with all the minions chiming in with oohs and aahs.

"Y'all are something else. If you must know, he's an attorney, his firm is a new client of Black Out"

"You seem to be in popular demand these days Ms. Braxton"

"Popular demand? How so? And if y'all don't stop!"

"Don't think that we didn't notice the guy who came here a few weeks ago. Y'all were real familiar," Oh so Chels wants some too…

"Not in popular demand ladiesssss. That was an old friend and this attorney is a client, meaning off limits! Okay?"

"Well I mean it has been a while since you've been out..." *Oh so y'all gone try me today, after I hugged y'all... Just raggedy. I get no respect.*

"That's not the point." They bundle my stuff up and put the painting in the car. I'm sure they're hoping I'll go entertain him, but joke's on them.

"Well, thank you ladies for the beautiful surprise and for closing tonight and no thank you for trying me! Ha, I will see you ladies tomorrow. Smooches."

"You need to be smooching one of them guys." Chels is in rare form tonight.

"You know wha-"

Smiling like a child trying to get out of trouble, she interjects. "I'm just playin'!"

"Mmhmm, I bet. Bye!" *I can't believe these heffas.*

Once I get in my house, on a high from the unexpected events this night entailed, all I can do is smile. I was going to hang up the painting, but then I decided against it. The way I'm set up right now, I'd tear up my wall and the painting would hang unevenly. I do however partake in some leftover cake while I respond to what's on my neglected social media profiles until I can scroll no longer. The Kitchen will have abbreviated hours tomorrow and the other offices will be closed for Indigenous Gathering and Negro Spiritual Day, so I am taking a road trip to Cleveland. Since our immediate family is so small, we alternate between going to see Cleveland family and hosting for this holiday. I think Danielle is tagging along, but I'm leaving when I say I am.

…

A few sing-alongs and inappropriate jokes later and we have arrived and are reunited with loving faces. With the amount of food Aunt Maya has cooked, this one day has to count as two cheat days. I should be ashamed of myself. *But I'm not!* All I hear are people talkin' that stuff, playing bid-whist, and reminiscing on back in the day while music fills the atmosphere. It's nearly two o'clock in the morning, and the party's still going. My dad just made more eggnog, but I think it's about that time for me to go to bed. I can barely keep my eyes open. My cousins are all up, but I can see they're winding down. We all are out here bringing glory to the Nash family name, so naturally it's past all of our bedtimes. *I gotta build up to all-nighters. I ain't as spry as I used to be. Shucks, was I ever really spry?* The old folks are the main ones wide awake. It's still surreal to me that my parents' generation make up the new old heads. Even though my parents were older when they had me, I never really saw them as old, but growing older and having been in a position to help them care for my ailing grandparents did make me want to have children younger than they were when they had me. None of us truly know what the future holds and God-forbid my parents become ill, but if they do someday require care, I don't want my kids to feel obligated to take care of them. I would want them to have the relationship with them they should. My hope is that Walt and Nita just grow older, stay reasonably healthy, and remain poppin'. That may be idealistic, but a girl can hope.

...

I miss being around family and not having to be the one in control all the time. Sometimes I miss just being Lil Walter like my great uncle called me... He's the one who recognized that entrepreneurial spirit in eight-year-old me. *"Back in the day when I was young I'm not a kid anymore but some days I sit and wish I was a kid again"*... Crap! I have to find something to wear for tomorrow. I go to the studio. I totally forgot. In the contract, we put that I'd do clusters of filming to shoot at a time so it wouldn't interfere too much in my supposedly hectic schedule. I think we will shoot two to three episodes tomorrow. I'm happy I booked afternoons; when we scheduled this weekend I had totally forgotten that it was our turn to drive since they came to

Detroit last time. I surely have not yet left the Land. We're all supposed to be going to dinner and then for drinks. I think I'll just drive out in the morning giving myself enough time to go figure out what I'm wearing and deal with glam.

...

Unfortunately, there were some hiccups with shooting today, I don't know if it was the nerves that I still haven't completely mastered or what. *It could be that I'm just friggin' ti'ed, but when am I not?* Maybe I just didn't drink enough water. I don't think I met my gallon yesterday. Whatever the problem was, after finally wrapping up enough footage for two episodes, I had one goal and that was to get in my bed. I hate to run the risk of sulking, it's just an off day and I'm learning to extend myself some grace, so comfort food it is. *Note to self, not a ticket to Glutton Town.*

Ah, Christmas in November is something to smile about. While I watch corny, sappy new holiday films and transition to classics, I try to ease my mind. I force myself to stop thinking in work mode and just focus on being content, peaceful, and still in this moment. I fight the urge to check my emails that are piling high. I had alerted staff not to contact me unless it was an extreme emergency and I haven't gotten a call, so everything must be fine. I haven't heard from my mentees in a while, maybe I should call them? *Maybe I should enjoy this predictable movie and chill out? Yeah, I'm right. I'll check in on them tomorrow.*

...

Getting ready for the day, I am determined to be better than yesterday. I prayed so hard this morning. *I prolly get on the Lord's nerves sometimes 'cause I be talkin' His ears off I'm sure.* Riding to the complex, I am gearing up to be mad productive. I'm hitting all of the offices today for some year-end meetings and regular updates. The girls should be fine at the café, so I'll stop there last to check in and make sure all of the new inventory came in on time. When I walked in my office, all of the messages piling up on my desk reminded me that my sweet, sweet Haley has left for South Carolina. They aren't quite emergent but this stack is borderline ridiculous.

I dive in and have to High-Five myself! I addressed everything on this desk in less than two hours, just in time for the meetings to start. Finally, as I put the phone down and look up, I see Meaghan standing in my door with a mischievous grin on her face holding a beautiful floral arrangement. It's been years since anyone has sent me flowers. I'm not much of a flowers type of chick, but the sentiment is nice and they are quite pretty. If I had to choose a favorite, it would probably be an orchid, any kind of orchid really, and it looks like these are lilies and orchids.

"Flowers, boss… And there's a card, too."

"I see…" Surely looking a bit perplexed, I leave my hand out as she holds the card with great excitement.

"Shall, we read it aloud?" She says almost singing her words and playfully dangles this note card in front me.

"Mmmm Miss Thang, if you don't give me that!" Laughing, she takes the card out as if she's going to try it, then hands it over.

As I read this card, I delight myself in her anxiety of wanting to know as she is beyond nosey for no reason. In honor of my petty crown, I stifle my reaction to the sender of this arrangement and aim to keep his identity secret from her to make her squirm. I place the card in my purse and look her in the face and simply say "It's about time for us to go to this meeting." She's so frustrated! It's hilarious! *Haaaa I won.*

When we walk out after wrapping up, I grab my purse.

"I'll grab those before I leave the complex."

"Who are they from?" She asks hopefully.

"Ooop, did you say something? I'm already in my next meeting. Sorry love."

"So you're just not going to tell me?!" *This is hilarious.*

"Nope," I say ever so sweetly walking past her.

I kept my word and accomplished everything on today's agenda. I truly get ecstatic when I check things off my schedule. *I really should get out more...* As I stop myself from working further, I think about the card Meag was dying to read. *"Ms. Braxton, you seem like a woman of manners, so I'll be expecting a call after you receive these. I hope you have a day as beautiful as you are. - James Lucas"*

I can't help but smile at how corny this is, but he is right about one thing, I am a woman of manners. Let me find his card. *Wait! What time is it? Gotta make sure it ain't creepin' into booty call hours.* I don't want to give his charmin' behind any ideas. Ah, it's only 8:30. That's not bad. I'll just call to say "thank you;" hopefully he doesn't answer, and I can leave a quick message.

Why is my heart pounding while this phone rings as if I'm a teenager calling a boy for the first time? I'm a grown woman calling a man to thank him for the flowers and remind him that I do not fraternize with my clients.

"Hello."

"Hi Mr. Lucas, this is Braxton."

"Ah, I was expecting your call."

"I'm sure, as you made a note of it. I also sense a bit of arrogance."

"Now, Ms. Braxton, if I didn't know any better, I'd think that you were unimpressed by my confidence."

"Regardless of that. Thank you for the lovely arrangement, but I must remind you that I don't make a habit of mingling with clients in my personal life."

"You and I both know that there's a first for everything. How about this? You let me take you out, just this once and then you can decide if you want to 'fraternize' or not," he says, sounding sure of himself.

"Mmm, I don't know."

"Just one time. Please?" *Did he just say please?* "If you don't, I'll just have to keep sending you stuff until you do."

"You can't buy my time with flowers."

"I can't, but I also peeped you have nosey employees who will no doubt badger you constantly about the handsome mystery man sending you all of those flowers."

"That's despicable and it's basically blackmail! And if you're a mystery how would they know if you're handsome?"

"Yeah, but the choice is yours. And they'd just guess" *Wow, this man might be crazy for real.*

"I will not be blackmailed, Mr. Lucas."

"Then just enjoy your flowers or other gifts. Have a good night."

This nigga ought to be ashamed of himself! "Wait, wait, wait! There's no need to send anything else," I say severely annoyed.

As fun as today was messin' with Meaghan at the office, I really don't need associates getting the wrong idea. As familial as I've made the culture, it still needs to have professionalism. Plus everyone does not need to know that a client is the sender because I will not have any mess with employees mingling with clients either. I might be the boss, but I have to lead by example.

...

This very well might be blackmail, but it's just dinner. *I guess.*

"So tell me about yourself." *Here we go…*

"There's not much to tell," I say matter-of-factly.

"I have a hard time believing that," he rubs his chin as he looks at me gauging if I'll share more.

"Hey Evangelist K!" I look around trying to find the face to match the familiar voice, then I see one of the new members of the church. She was at the women's meeting last week. She is so sweet, which makes my forgetting her name even worse. I'm terrible at names in the beginning and I forgot she said she works here.

"Hey girl! How you doin'?"

"I'm fine and you?"

"I'm alright, thanks. I forgot you said you work here. It's nice to see you!"

"Thanks, same here! I didn't want to interrupt. I just wanted to say hi. See you Sunday."

"See you Sunday! Have a good one."

It's always weird when my worlds collide. I don't get too personal with a lot of people, even at my church. I'm always gone be me and I don't pretend to be someone I'm not in any environment, but as a minister I have to be careful in how personal I get. I always have to walk the line of being transparent and reachable while remaining private. I'm not out here living a whole other life, but a lot of people look for any reason to discredit what preachers preach, so I take precautions to minimize their opportunities, like I don't pretend I don't drink, but I also don't publicize it. The first thing that flies out of some people's mouths is "ain't you a preacher"… *Mmmm yeah playboy.* I don't drink to excess. I do not have an addiction. Someone once told me "you haven't been delivered yet;"she was an ex-alcoholic. I've needed deliverance of many things, and still do in various areas, but that was not one of them. I only do Bible studies with people over trivial matters when necessary because many want to argue. I don't argue the Bible. When I'm asked, I typically answer questions and back them with the Word. It's kind of my calling after all, but I don't entertain those who seek to engage in fruitless fights. People talk about the height of my heels and how unholy they are or the fact that when it's hot I typically don't wear pantyhose or how I wear pants in the pulpit or how I have a tattoo or how I look the wrong way, blah blah blah. People find any reason, even those without merit, to try to discredit me 'cause such is life, but I go through great lengths to practice what I preach. I don't do the clique thing, but because of that I do have to set clear boundaries with some members, especially those whose intentions are unproven. Of course I have closeness with my church family. I do make it a point to treat them like family because that's what we are. We are here to support one another, but sometimes due to the nature of my position, I have to provide more support than I receive where I am planted.

"So you're a minister, too?"

"Yes, yes I am. I typically don't tell people off the bat that I'm a preacher. I prefer my lifestyle to speak for itself rather than telling everyone how saved I am. I normally let my position in ministry unfold naturally." *I am lowkey guilty of using it as a weapon to not talk to men when I don't want to be bothered. Dang! I should've used that this time! Shucks, but it doesn't work everytime.*

"Dang, lady! What don't you do?"

"A lot."

"So what is that like? Preaching and stuff?"

"Preaching is crazy. There's nothing like it really. Those who don't understand think I'm insane talkin' supernatural mumbo jumbo. Out of all of my gifts, preaching often takes precedence."

As the night goes on, I realize we indeed have a lot in common. Maybe he's not as arrogant as I thought. He too is a product of Detroit Public Schools, and he grew up hood adjacent, too! Apparently, he grew up like a zip code away from me, but he's a tad older. What was really great is that as far as I can tell, he is the Biblical definition of a Christian, too.

As he walks me to my car, we continue to chat for a moment. We say our goodnights and he walks away once my car starts. I glance over to see him to his, then I drive off and head home. When I finally am around the corner, not *around the corner when I'm on my way to pick up one of my girls, but like real life around the corner,* the best "get-out" song came on, "Single" by Natasha Bedingfield. That was my jam! *I really wanna know what young me was going through, but this was a bop! I mean I was too young to date, of course I was single! I really be crackin' myself up.*

When I walk in the house, I review my to-do lists for tomorrow before winding down, and my phone buzzes. I forgot it was still on vibrate.

9:56pm "Home safe?"

9:59pm "Yes, you?"

...

When I finish my morning prayer, meditation, and workout, I begin to prepare myself for the day. As I look in the mirror trying to decide if I'm wearing a wash-n-go or riding out my straightened hair for another day, a smile goes across my lips. *James Lucas.* As nice as last night was, it was a one-time deal. I think it's best to keep things professional.

Oh shoot! Rosalind! I totally forgot that we have a scheduled home visit today. I hope I find out what my people have told her, but I'm not sure if she's allowed to share those details. I think we are going over some of the training for dealing with trauma. Some of these babies have been exposed to unimaginable circumstances and whoever my baby is may have experienced some. Even though I'm planning on adopting, I'm getting my license to foster to really boost my approval odds. My mom came over as Rosalind was leaving. I could tell she was holding back whatever she wanted to express.

"Mommy, what is it?"

"Are you sure you aren't rushing into this?" *Here we go. I try to suppress a long sigh.*

"I didn't decide this overnight." I'm trying so hard to watch my tone because she's my mom, but I'm not dependent on her and Daddy like I was when they could overrule certain decisions. I'm tired of having this same conversation.

"I know sweetie, but look at yourself. I can see that you're exhausted right now. You barely spend time at home because you're out being the Minnie Mogul all the time. You only slow down when your body shuts down and you have no choice."

"My health has taken a lot from me and you more than anyone else know that. I promised myself that I wasn't going to allow my health to dictate my life. I wasn't going to accept the constraints that doctors and research attempted to put on me. You didn't raise me to let them have the last word."

"But you're so young and you have time. You gotta walk in wisdom and know and adapt to your limits. That's not quitting! And didn't you go on a date last night? You thought I wouldn't notice. Being a single mother will make dating harder than it already is, since you so mean to the fellas."

"It was just dinner and I don't think it's going any further."

"Why not?"

"I just don't and I'm in the middle of the adoption process. I'm not complicating that."

"Maybe that's a reason to slow it down…"

"Mommy, I owe you and Daddy everything, but I'm not asking permission. If I'm approved I will be somebody's mom. I have to go be the Don In Heels. Believe it or not, I listen to you and Daddy, not just hear you, but I have to do what I believe is right. I love you, Momma. I'll talk to you later. "

What's annoying about Nita basically being my best friend is that when I'm frustrated with her, it doesn't last long. I can never stay mad at her. *I'm not per se mad at her. I'm just frustrated.* How is it that they raised me to do work beyond my situation and do whatever I put my mind to, then try to talk me out of something I've been wanting and working toward for so long?

I work incessantly because I never know when I can't or when I'll be out of commission for days, maybe even weeks, or over a month at a time. I've been down for months before. I've been working so hard because I want there to be something left. *Only what you do for Christ lasts…* I find enjoyment in ministry and business. I don't make ministry business, but I do make my business a part of ministry. I know that my labor is not in vain. I know I need to make more time for a life and not just work, work, work and no play, but I'm fighting to see through this vision that has been imprinted in my mind for so long. I'm fighting to live on purpose. I'm fighting to build something bigger than me, but now I'm fighting to have someone to leave it to. Even if she doesn't want it, she'll have a choice. My corporation is my baby. It's a gift that I birthed, and I want it to grow even after I'm gone because it's much more than me, or even if I decide to actually retire one day and not do this forever. Whatever the case, I've been working for the well-being and future of my children, and I haven't even met them yet.

...

By the time I make it back home, I don't fully know what all I did today. Well whatever it was, I sure hope it was productive. I'm scheduled to go to the café tomorrow to wrap up this chef's menu. It went on for a little longer than normal. It went over so well that I may add the most popular items to the regular menu. After today, I may take it easy *or try* until the twelve days of Christmas brunches and family dinners. We are relatively prepared for that, and Michele and Samantha have everything under control. I'll just need a couple days because I have to listen to my body before it starts to really show out.

...

Thank God! Closing time has come. It was a busy day, but we had a successful wrap of the chef's menu. We got a new regular this month, but I don't think I've ever been so excited to see my truck so that I could go home to wash off the day and get in my bed. I don't even know if I ate today, but I'm too tired to care. Only Jesus knows how I'm still walking around as much as my body is cussing me clean out...

I missed my bed and somehow ended up on the floor. I'm too weak to pick myself up. As I have no more fight left in me at this moment in time, I lay here on my plush spacious area rug and use all my might to drag my duvet on the floor to wrap myself up like a taco. *Oooh tacos would have been great. I don't think there's a day that goes by when I don't want tacos.* I hear my phone going off with multiple texts, but I can't get to it quite yet. If it's important whoever it is will call and I don't feel anything in my spirit. Soon I'm in a half-sleep state. I'm slightly awake, but I can't open my eyes. By the time I'm able to come to, it's six in the morning. I miraculously get myself off of the floor, climb in my bed and grab my phone. I glance at my phone and see that Mr. Lucas has texted me and CJ. My sisterfriend will be in town. Her crazy self will be coming over tomorrow, *well today.* I decide to text back James Lucas later and tarry for sweet sleep even if only for a little while.

I get up moving slowly but I have some work I need to tend to before she comes. Thankfully, what I need to do can get done from home. CJ always makes herself at home, which makes it easier for me because I don't have to do much as far as entertaining. It took her a while to figure out what she actually wanted to do, but she really is making a name for herself as a midwife. She is also a wonderful mother to my precious niece and nephew, Joelle and Joey. I love me some them. *Baby fever be comin' in waves. Oh my ovaries. They need to chill.*

"Hey boo!"

"Sup my baby!"

"How are you?"

"I'm good, tryna be like you when I grow up. Look at this house!"

"Well thank you, but girl bye I've seen where you live honey, trust you're doing just fine"

"I haven't seen you in forever. You gotta catch me up."

While we catch up, I get so excited to hear how well she's doing. My friends are really out here being great. Nothing is perfect, but in this season, there is wellness, coping with life, and walking in gratitude. That's so dope to see. When she asks what's new with me, I contemplate telling her about the adoption process. As she briefs me on her mom and everybody, suddenly I'm shutting down. My vision is blurry, and Dumbo has taken a seat on my chest. I'm burning hot.

> "Kenny, are you okay? You don't look so good."

> "I'm straight."

> "Maybe you just need some rest." *Rest? Rest!*

I don't know why, but that word often arouses extreme frustration within me. People have been telling me to *rest* for quite some time. It's typically the same ones who know the deal but still ask "what's wrong" every time I verbalize that I don't feel well. If I actually say the words, then it is clear that it's a bad day. They tell me to rest as if a nap will make chronic illnesses disappear. I've heard the word utilized as a command all too many times this week alone and hearing it now is the boisterous clash of cymbals that sets off the alarm. *I often wanna tell all of 'em "No, nigga you rest!" but that's not the Christian thing to do...* When you have health issues, people always have an opinion, some unwarranted and unsolicited advice, or a terrible story to tell. People love stories. That's why I live my life with the motto of not looking how I feel because it's nobody's business, and I don't want to hear "Oh my aunt had that, but it turned into lupus or my mom had that and it got worse when she got pregnant or blah blah blah. I got tired of people judging me for deciding not to live in bed half the time and hearing people tell me just to *rest!* But that surely doesn't beat the condescending "maybe it's in your head" "maybe you're pessimistic and too negative and that's why treatments haven't really worked." Then there are some who say "so you're just not going to do anything" as if what I experience is not real. *I'd like nothing more than to tell them "f*** you and your thoughts too," but again not the saved thing to do, so I keep it to myself and mind my business.*

It took every ounce of patience in my being not to take all of my rage out on CJ. She just got here, and she's concerned about me. Rest is logical, but it is layered. She ain't the type to be malicious or patronizing to me. She just has eyes to see I'm not okay. I am very much not okay. I will my body to fall in line and schedule a dinner with CJ before she leaves town then I see her out. As I close the door, I catch myself from falling and ease myself onto the floor. I sit there until I'm confident that I can make it upstairs. *I'm quite over this.* Crawling into my bed, it dawns on me that I have failed to respond to a message… After I do that, maybe I will finally get some rest. Some days I'm better at pacing myself than others. I'm trying to embody that sometimes for the show to go on, the show has to pause. I know that sometimes I must rest, as everyone does, but sometimes it infuriates me that I have to rest after a daily task is done. Sometimes it angers me that my body can shut down even while sitting catching up with one of my oldest friends.

There are times when people thought I felt good because I was dancing, laughing, being the life of the party. In reality, in those times my body has often still felt on fire. I could just move on those days. A few of them may actually have been good, minimal symptoms, but those days have been rare. Many of them have been awful internally. I was just able to give the illusion that my body was not getting in jab after jab. I was laughing and dancing being the life of the party as a reminder that I won't yield to this invisible nemesis that always shows up to muck up my day. Sometimes it feels like it wins, but I fight harder when I have the strength. Even when I am resting, often this Storybrooke villain keeps going. Maybe that's why rest can be hard, such a layered concept for me, because I don't want to give it a chance to one up me. *Only God can help me understand. Lord, please lead me. I don't want to kill myself trying to fight what ails me.*

In between meetings, I see that James Lucas has asked me out again... *Didn't we just go out? My days run together, but I'm pretty sure it's barely been a week.* The only way I can justify this is if it is business related.

After I wrap up for the day, music drives me home. As I'm pulling into my driveway, CoCo calls. I haven't spoken to her all week, which is odd. I can hear her excitement to come back home in her voice and as I'm getting out of my car, she asks how my date was. *Nita!*

"Yo Step-Momma told you I went out the other night?"

"You know she did."

"Ugh, it was fine, but it was a one-time thing. He's a client."

"She didn't tell me that."

"Cause she doesn't know that and the less she knows about him the better. He asked me out again for this week, but I'm not going unless it's business related."

"How come?!"

"Didn't you just hear me say he's a client!
That could potentially be messy, and I
don't do messy so issa no for me dawg!"

"Girl bye, if you don't quit playin'!"

"You quit playin'."

After we finish talking and I finally walk in the
house, I sit at the breakfast bar in my kitchen
thinking maybe she's right, and I don't like that.
She better not tell Mommy that he's a client. I
don't need that line of questioning. *I guess it
won't hurt...* Against my first mind, I acquiesced.

"So how did you become such a
household name in the community?"

"Is this an interview?" I ask.

"Maybe. It's only fair. You know what I do
and how I came about. I still don't see
how you became a lawyer."

"Ha and what's that supposed to mean?"

"Not like that, but how did you manage to
build businesses while getting a law
degree?"

"Well, I started Dope and Black Out
during undergrad. I never liked school,
but I was usually good at it until college.
Then as I was closer to finally being

finished, I contemplated if I would even go to grad school. I couldn't stomach paying even more money and investing more time in something I didn't even want. I always believed that education didn't have to be formal to be valid and I still stand by that, but something dawned on me that it was the right move and another step to invest in myself and my brand, so I did. Somewhere around senior year of undergrad I started Braxton Holdings Inc. and bridged my businesses together. I studied for the LSAT to get into a dual JD and MBA program, my hobby became official and Kenny's Kitchen was born, then I hired my first employees so I could focus on school and catering. I went to school year-round to finish the accelerated program. I actually just passed the Bar at the beginning of this year, and the storefront of Kenny's Kitchen Café is about six months old. The rest is history. Aaannnd clearly you didn't ask for all that, but yeah there's that and I'm done rambling now."

"And you forgot to mention your new show." *Somebody does research, but then again research is the life of a lawyer.*

"It's just a local show, but I must admit it is pretty dope." *I laugh because it's what Grey would call "broke nigga tv."*

...

Waking up, it is clear that I won't be visiting my punching bag, Dr. Everlast, this morning. It's still early so I take extra time in my meditation in the Word and prayer. The offices are pretty slow, so I'll go in tomorrow. I think I'm only leaving the house today to run personal errands. It's quite novel for me to actually do stuff for my household exclusively and not finding some way to mix in work. I'm beginning to believe people when they say that I work too much. *Meh.*

I was moving a bit slow today, and apparently it was very noticeable for someone my age. It was so noticeable that some old lady whom I have never met felt compelled to tell me, "You're too young to move that slow, honey." Instead of telling her the story of how I was first told I had a health history of someone three times my age when I was eighteen years old and to mind her own cuss word business, I simply said "Well, it would appear so. Have a nice day ma'am." Audacious people should be thankful that I was raised right. I wish it would dawn on them that they don't actually know the stories of the strangers they pass on the street because THEY'RE STRANGERS! *How do you know I'm*

*moving slow today if you don't know how I
regularly move?! I mean it was slow today as I
normally strut in pumps, but that's not the point.*
It would be different if it was something obvious
like sagging too much with a belt on or wearing
leggings without covering your behind when
underwear or lack thereof is visible. Stuff like that
I can understand, but even those have exceptions.
It's always the old people who try me the most.

By the time I get back and do a few chores around
the house, I'm tired and about ready for my
movies. *I could read a book instead. I'll play it by
ear.* When I sit down and pick up my phone, I
respond to a few emails and then a message from
James Lucas. I think I'll call him Luke. *Yeah, that'll
work.* I know my plan changed from just once to
only twice and now I don't know, but he is
persistent. I've seen him a couple times in the last
couple weeks. The light knock on my door
interrupts my revelries.

"Hey Baby Girl, can I come in?" *I forgot my
parents were coming today.*

"Yes, I'm decent. Hey Daddy."

"How you feelin'?"

"I'm tired, but I'm okay. How are you?"

"I'm okay, but you gotta take it easy."

"I know… I've just had a lot of work to do lately."

"I know, but you gotta make sure you're feeling okay especially since Mommy and I aren't always here."

"I'm fine Daddy. I promise. It's good that you and Mommy aren't always here so that y'all aren't worrying about me all the time. I'm a big girl now, Dad. I'm okay." I'm actually happy that they're here for Christmas. Having Christmas at home reminds me of when we were kids before Mommy moved out because of the roller coaster her and Daddy were on, it was just the four of us. Then the both of them taking care of their moms became our reality. It was always a lot going on, but now we seem to have more peace collectively. *For that I am grateful.*

I thought this was somehow going to segue into the discussion of adoption, but Daddy has said the least about it since our initial conversation, which doesn't make sense. Even though Mommy is my voice of reason a lot of times, Daddy is too. I'm more like him in all honesty. He still shows me when I'm a little off or just plain out-of-line. Most of the time, I listen to him. Right now, he's the voice I want to hear, but at the same time I don't because I wouldn't know what to do if he tried to talk me out of it. Walt always wanted me to do great things, but he was also apprehensive because he never wanted me to tire myself out. *I don't really need to do much to tire myself out.* I think at times my strength and capacity would surprise yet impress him. He always wanted to protect me, as good fathers do for their children, but some things he couldn't fix.. I remember one night during a really fierce flare up when my left side went out for the second time, it was virtually temporary paralysis. I was on the couch. I couldn't fathom going back upstairs solely relying on my right side for stability, so I slept on the couch after he and I watched superhero movies and ate pizza. Daddy, my superhero, slept in the oversized beige leather chair to make sure I was okay. At first, I didn't realize why he was downstairs so late, then it dawned on me that he knew I wasn't okay, so he was not leaving me alone even if just a few stairs were in between us. My dad was always there to save the day, even though he knew sometimes saving the day was not stopping me from living my life, but supporting me to push the limits. Much to my ambivalence, we did not talk about the elephant in the room, but instead I talked him into watching a 'Transformers' movie. This is nice. As a child, I didn't regularly get to spend much time with him. He worked tirelessly and then for a while I didn't live in the same house as my dad all the time. I see him more as an adult than I did as a child.

> "I'm serious now, you gotta wait 'til you're feeling all the way better to go out. I used to call Daddy when it was really humid or cold to tell him not to go outside. I think it's too cold outside for you right now," he says, remembering the severity of George Shunger's breathing troubles.

I already decided that I was staying in for the rest of the day. I haven't felt all the way better in Lord knows how long. Instead of expressing any of this, I simply resolve...

"Okay Daddy, I won't."

My dad's biggest concern is my breathing, not the twenty other things that go wrong, but it frightens him because George Shunger and Tee both died from COPD. It's just that sometimes asthma and its broke cousin bronchitis pray on my downfall. The combination with the long-lost relatives can make some days really trying. Tee and George Shunger both knew they were sick but didn't say anything, so he gets quite upset when I keep things to myself. The irony of it is that I do it for them. In this case, it's not for my sense of privacy, it's for their protection so that they don't worry to death. It's funny because I get equally peeved when they try to keep things from me. I'm very vehement about their well-being. When Daddy had to have surgery, I told him "I'll take care of you," and he assured me "We'll take care of each other." That's what we do, and sometimes me taking care of them is not telling them every little detail and dragging them, mainly my mom, to every important appointment.

I had to stop venting so much to my mom. She spent the most time with me during severe flare ups, but one day it hit me like a ton of bricks to retreat. But I always needed her and still do. We're disturbingly codependent. She used to assure me that everything was going to work out and I was going to get everything I worked for and that God had it all under control. But the more I saw the weight in her eyes, the less I believed. She told me I was the strongest person she knew so I had to be strong for her…and him.

After an afternoon with Optimus Prime and Bumblebee, Walt goes to meet Nita. They're the cutest. *Goin' on dates and stuff. It's kinda gross, but they're adorable. I love seeing them in this element now. I get to see what little me didn't see growing up.*

It's about that time for me to wind down and get into my nightly routine. With the youth service I have to preach at coming up in about a week or so, I need to start preparing myself. The worst thing to do is to procrastinate on studying and preparing for preaching. The last time waiting for delayed greatness backfired on me was the day I learned my lesson. I had Kelsey that night and I thought I had an idea for a sermon, but then God was like nah. I didn't know what I was preaching until mere hours before service and that was the one time that I did not feel the presence of God while delivering the Message. I surely learned, so even if He changes it last minute, I take advantage of all of the allotted time. Studying regularly also helps. *You gotta put something in to get something out.*

Reflecting on yesterday's assignment at the youth service, I am grateful that I still get nervous every time I am set to preach. The nervousness doesn't stem from questioning my own ability, but being sure I am moved out of the way and not depending on *my* own ability. Also, it allows me to be certain that I am being led by the Holy Spirit. The nervousness is acknowledging that I have a responsibility. I never want to take it lightly whenever and however God chooses to use me. If there ever comes a time when I am not nervous before I have a preaching assignment, I pray I feel the conviction hit before it's too late…

Shaking off the exhaustion, I head to headquarters for more meetings. In this arena, there are little to no reasons for nervousness. Sometimes I miss actually being out in the field and the adrenaline that comes from making ish happen for clients, but this is cool too. As I prepare to call in my team, suddenly, something is stopping me in my tracks. *It's happening again.* The pressure, pain, weight consumes me, takes my breath away, blurs my vision, and seizes my head clouding my entire body and taking me down to the floor. I end up under my desk. Piper walks into my office. *Crap!*

"Ms. Braxton, I just wanted- wait, are you okay?"

I am barely able to form words, but I manage to faintly let out, "I'm fine, please give me a minute."

"Are you sure? You don't look so good."

"I'm sure," I say, concentrating on breathing.

"Ms. Bra-" Her voice is frantic, but I cut her off before she can continue.

"GET OUT!" The last ounce of strength I had in that moment was used to yell; I probably scared her, but I don't have time to address that right now. I struggle to bring life back to my face and steady myself on my feet. I straighten up and walk tall in my stilettos like nothing happened. When I leave, I tell Meaghan the team meeting is pushed and to hold my calls and to text me whatever meetings I have left that she can't regretfully postpone for me. Piper sees me as I walk forward with tunnel vision with only the mission of staying afloat. She flushes as I walk by her on the way to the door. Meaghan calls me about an hour later with what I'll have to personally address. She then mentions Piper.

"Has she signed her NDA?" I ask pointedly.

"Yes"

"Good." Privacy has been a nonexistent concept in America for Lord knows how long, but the shred of privacy I have I will keep. The bigger this small business gets, the harder that is.

Sometimes I do feel like a superhero. But it feels like the strength is a hoax, a mask that I put on, an elaborate scheme I've been orchestrating. Rather my true identity is weak and feeble. I don't always know when to wear the mask or when to take it off, when to push through or when to recalibrate or to just be still and let myself recuperate and prepare for the next battle against my arch nemesis. I try to absorb the Son, but sometimes I get ahead of myself and miss that step. *That misstep causes the hardest fall. I think it's called pride. Most days I feel like I have something to prove all while trying to beat the clock in Kitchen Stadium.*

Being needed can become an addiction, not always because one wants it. Some people crave power so they see being needed by someone as having power over that person. That's not what I consciously want. *Who knows what our hearts seek unconsciously, our hearts deceive us….* Since childhood, I've often attached my value based upon being needed, being useful. I did not always see value in who I am, better yet Whose I am. It was always about what I could do for someone. I suppose that trait has not really left yet. Because of that, I admittedly have a problem being seen as weak, needy, useless, unreliable -unworthy. Even sick, if there's even a speck of a possibility for me to do it, I work, I serve.

...

After I lay down for a bit, I go through my to-do list. It's amazing all the work I get done from my bed. For the meetings that cannot wait, I schedule video conferencing for tomorrow morning. With so much year-end stuff, I'm happy I only have one more taping for the show left for the year, and that's perfect because that'll be the only work I'm allowed to do with a full house. When I'm shutting my laptop down for the night, my mom strolls in my room. *It's my house and still she doesn't knock, but then again I only knock when Daddy's in the room. Where are our boundaries? We really need some.*

"Hey baby baby."

"Hey girlfriend, how you doin'?"

"I'm okay, how are you?" She asks with *that* look.

"I'm fine."

"You don't look like it." *Well thanks for that.*

"I'm okay."

"When are you going to stop working yourself ragged?"

"I'm fine! Mommy I told you I'm a superhero. Superheroes can do super stuff, so being super sick is just a price to pay for all of my poppin' super-ness! I'm just tryna be the business mogul and the vigilante Detroit needs, Mommy." Before looking back at her to finish this rerun, I see "Hey Boss Lady" come up on my screen.

"And who has you smiling?"

"Huh?"

"Don't you huh me. Who is that?"

"Mom, you know I get excited when I start talking superheroes. I was thinking about watching Luke Cage again. Who doesn't want to see a Black man with impenetrable skin."

"Mmhmmm"

Mommy wouldn't be my homegirl if she wasn't all in my business. She doesn't need to know about this young man right now.

...

After my meetings, I sigh in relief that I am so close to a semi staycation. Danielle is riding with me to pick up CoCo at the airport. The festivities shall begin. I made the first batch of eggnog last night. Tonight, we shall watch 'Grandma Got Ran Over By a Reindeer' like we used to with Mama.

Surprisingly we have no ornament casualties thus far even with at least two strippers in everybody's nog. We come from a clumsy family and apparently one full of jokes too…

> "Yeah cause Kendall the wrong mutha effa to eff wit…. She went from Kenny to Walt in point two seconds," Dani says with a hearty laugh.

> "That white lady at the dress shop had me messed up and you know it! And you must be some kin to Moonie always bringin' up that old ish Dani! Ain't nobody ask you nothin! You cut off, no mo drank fa you!" I say laughing, sticking my tongue out.

In hopes of having a life tomorrow night, we made a pact to get up at a decent hour so we can make Mama's original five Christmas cookies. It'll be a nice change being done early and not staying up until the wee hours of the night. Maybe we'll do something festive or not..

With just a few days left until Christmas, I check in with the offices to make sure all of the year-end events are cool, and I totally forgot about the Braxton Holdings Inc. party! Looks like I have no choice but to go out tomorrow.

...

Tonight is the night when all of Braxton Holdings Inc. comes together to celebrate. Many of our clients, vendors, and a few other local business people of the community join in the festivities as well. The family comes when they're in town, and it looks like they'll be coming today.

How I forgot about a whole event that my business is putting on I have no clue, but nonetheless I tell the fam; and about an hour later I have found my ensemble. *In a room full of plain black kitten heels, I am a red or printed stiletto.* At least today there's a reason for my extra-ness. Some fashion days, I like to think I'm like the Black, saved Carrie Bradshaw. Unlike the family, I cannot take my sweet time and be fashionably late for this occasion, so I head up to my boudoir to get ready. With my music blasting, I hop in a glorious shower, and find the perfect paint to put on this face. Finally I step into an amethyst gown with jeweled sheer long sleeves. I've been waiting for a reason to wear this. I bought it a few months ago because I fell in love when I saw it. It's nice not having to wait for another check to come in to buy something and just treat myself every now and then. As nice as this dress is, I'm pretty sure the shoes are winning. They're gold pointed-toe stilettos with hints of champagne, which goes perfectly with my clutch purse. I can't help but queue "Bossy" by Kelis.

My song is interrupted by a very important phone call. *My handsome boy!*

"Hi Auntie's big boy! How are you?"

"Good, you?"

"I'm better now that I hear from my handsome boy! Are you being good?"

"Yes, can I come over?"

"I would love that, but Auntie has to go work tonight. How about I pick you up tomorrow?"

"Yay!" The excitement in his voice still gets me. Gosh, this kid has been trying to make me soft since I laid eyes on him as a little baby. I guess it is about time I get Kelsey. It is his turn. I got my other baby boy Ken by himself last time. I try to be fair with the rotation.

Finally, I head onward to the party. It was a bit of a stretch, but we were able to make it happen and fit the party at my other house. I have an inkling that next year it'll be too large for the house to accommodate. It's shaping up to be a gala extravaganza. As the party gets started and my employees enjoy being waited on instead of working for a change, some clients come strolling in. It didn't hit me until I saw his face that he may be here…*Yup, cause no. This ain't gone work.* As my family shows up looking right if I do say so, I know that I need to keep them busy so that they receive no unnecessary information. I have to keep an eye on whom they're mixing and mingling with. *Oh Lawd, I've been cornered.*

> "Ms. Braxton, are you avoiding me?" *He real fione tuhday! He betta gone somewhere.*

> "Of course not, it's just a busy night for me."

> "Mmhmm, I see, well you look gorgeous." *I still have a hard time believing that to be true when people say it.*

> "Well thank you, you clean up nice yourself."

> "You can go back to 'working' if you must…" *He tried it!*

> "Did you just air quote at me as if I'm not working?"

"It is a party."

"For the guests, yes, but this is still a business event."

Much to my relief I see Drew, the journalist, trying to get my attention. I catch up with him and make sure he has everything he needs for the story then we snap a few photographs. The photographer of the night is my cousin Jay. When I first built the website for Dope, she did the promo shoot pro bono. I'm not much of a photo person, but it comes with the territory. We have a gold carpet laid out where I'm forced to take too many pictures with nearly everyone, including James Lucas, Esq. *At least he knows some kind of discretion...* Meaghan still doesn't know that he sent those flowers, and no one knows he's the one I've been sort of seeing.

Tonight was a success, everyone had a good time. They even previewed some of the items that'll be featured for the special Christmas menu, which went over really well. Champagne, eggnog, and Apple Cider were flowing. People mingled, danced, and were merry, so it was all worth it. After I see off the event staff and lock up this house, I head to the crib.

When I get home, I see that I received a text from Luke, but I more importantly missed a call from Rosalind. She left a voicemail.

"Ms. Braxton. I've begun the interviewing process, but I need to set up interviews with your sister and a few other people in your support system. I'll be dropping by to do another visit with you soon, but it may be after the New Year. Happy Holidays."

When I scrub the paint off my face, I'm exhausted but somehow wide awake. I go to the den to watch tv and to no surprise I find CoCo and Dani. We crack open Mama's cookies and watch low-budget movies *ahh one of our favorite past-times.* When Dani goes to the guest room downstairs, CoCo and I chat before heading upstairs. I drop the bomb that Ms. Ferrell will be calling her soon to interview her, but it shouldn't be that much of a shock. I did tell her that this was a real thing two months ago.

I wonder how Kelsey will handle another baby in my life, even though he'd say "TeeTee I'm not a baby. I'm seven!" *Then I'll have to remind him that he will be a baby for as long as I say he is!* Our bond is ridiculous, so this may take a bit of adjusting. Shucks, he had to adjust when Ken came along because he's Auntie's baby, too.

....

When I drag myself out of bed, I can feel that today is going to be a fight, but my little boy asked to come over and darn it he's coming over! I never go backsies on my baby, except for when I absolutely have to, and I always make it up to him. If I can't keep my word to a child, then my word is nothing. After talking to Joyce, we head out for Auntie Kenny and Kels time. We stop at my surprisingly empty house before going on our adventure. I wonder where everyone ran. *They better not be having family fun without me.*

"Hey, you with the face."

"Yes?"

"What's the matter, kid? Who do I have to fight?"

"Nobody."

"No, tell me what's wrong."

He shrugs at me, not giving away much.

"Was it some kids? I'll fight some kids."

"TeeTee, you can't fight kids." Finally, I see a little smirk.

"Why not?!"

"Because you're a grown up."

"Oh okay, that makes sense, but I'll fight their parents." I just love his little laugh. I have to savor these fleeting days that getting him out of a funk will be as easy as play fighting with him. *I gotta stop rough-housing with him like he's still small and like I'm not old as all get out... I can't help but get those little cheeks.*

"There's that little face! Who can be mean to that wittle face, huh?! How long are you gonna let me have my cuddles and kisses before you're too cool for your favorite Auntie?"

"I don't know. Two more years maybe."

"Two more years?! That's it?! Well, are you too cool for our tradition? We're really late this year, so there's only a couple to choose from, but you can still pick an orchard from those.

"I know where I wanna go."

"Good! 'Cause we're about to go. Go get ready, kid." He usually talks on car rides, so I'll try to get to the bottom of it on the road. I need to see how serious it is and if I need to tell his mom.

When we get back, I revel in the moment that this little boy is fascinated by the little things, and try to plot how I'll break the news. Joyce agreed not to say anything until I talked to him first.

I suppose it is time to tell the girls and everyone else…

"TeeTee?"

"Yes, kid." As I look down at my handsome boy's face, he looks confused, which peaks my concern.

"Somebody said that you're not my real Auntie, is that true?"

"Of course not. I'm as real as they come, baby boy. What this 'somebody' said was not quite right, but your mommy and I aren't biological sisters."

"What's that mean?"

"We aren't blood sisters and there was no adoption or anything like that, but sometimes you get to choose your family." I am really not good at this. The confusion is written all over his face. *Who told my baby this?*

"Huh?"

"Your mommy met my sister many, many years ago then your mommy and I became friends, but we were more like family. I became your mommy's sister and when I finally laid eyes on you, you were 6 months and we were inseparable instantly. I was the first one to babysit you and the first person to keep you overnight outside of your Nana. So kid, we may not share blood, but you are my real nephew and I'll punch anyone who tells you otherwise."

"Auntie, what's adoption?" *Well, now's as good a time as any...*

"Well it's funny you ask that, adoption is when an adult or a family officially makes a kid who is not their biological child their baby. So it's kind of like what your mom and I did with each other as sisters, but it's matching parents with children. I am going to be adopting soon."

"You are?"

"Yes, I am. How would you feel about getting a new cousin?"

"Would you still be all mine?" *Oh my goodness!*

"Well, kind of, but it wouldn't just be me anymore. I would have a daughter just like your parents have you and Ken."

"But you don't have a husband?" *Well gee, thanks kid, obvious!*

"You want a snack?"

Well, a snack should distract him for a while before his mind circles back to this conversation. It was so much simpler when he was three when his best observation was "TeeTee, you're funny."

Who made him so inquisitive?! After I drop him off at home, I call Mia and tell her before she blows a gasket if I tell anyone else before her. Trust me, she'd know. So after some brief small talk, I dropped the bomb.

> "My mom has been telling me I'm going to be a good mom since forever, so hopefully I will in real life."

> "Well, you've only been taking care of people forever… You have a first aid kit, baby wipes, emergency snacks, and trash bags in your car! You've always been a mom," she says with conviction.

After we wrap up our conversation, I try to jump back into reality when Luke hits my line. He asked me to go out yesterday, but I had on my auntie hat. As I answer, he wears me down a bit and we apparently have plans a couple days after Christmas. *I feel like I should be more excited about him and his persistence than I actually am.*

…

March 08, 2022

He strolls into my office and demands my full attention without saying a word, making the tasks at hand mere distractions. This was not supposed to happen. Guilt consumes me because I haven't told him a word about this pending life-changing event. We've been going out for the past few months. I guess I could even say he's full-on courting me. I've never truly been "courted" before him. I think he just said something, but I have no idea what.

"Hellooooo."

"Huh?"

"You didn't hear a word I said, did you?"

"Yes, I did not," I say, trying to keep my composure.

"Are you still coming to my family dinner later?" He says, trying not to show his annoyance with me.

"I said yes." *That sounded less rude in my head.*

"But you have a habit of canceling at the last minute." *This is why I ain't wanna be bothered in the first place.*

"But you know I have reasons for why and for Pete's sake I said yes." *He needs to leave my office before this goes left for real. I'm really trying to work.*

It's obvious I'm getting frustrated, so I try to apologize for being snappy before he leaves. There's no need for this tension.

I do not want to meet this man's family, that makes things real. But now I'm locked in 'cause I ain't gone make a liar out of myself... Lord, what did I get myself into? I think I like him.

...

"You're the first lady James has brought to meet us since, well ever really, so I'm sure you're quite the lady. He's always so private."

"Thank you, Mrs. Lucas, I'm alright I suppose."

"Please Ma, let's not run her off." Luke interjects on my behalf and then scooches over closer to me on this adorable suede burnt orange loveseat. I must learn who their interior decorator is because we could use some work over at the compound. We haven't been there long. I'm still gradually adding pieces making it look and feel like a place people want to go to throughout the week. *Shucks, even when I'm not workin', I'm workin'. Be in the moment chick, dang!*

His father is even more surprised at my having esquire behind my name than his son was when we met. *Is something on my forehead or what?* I know this assumption can't be because I'm too nice. Eventually we find common ground on the unpopular views of the government. We had quite the conversation, but I can tell he's slightly chauvinistic; he doesn't even acknowledge female preachers. It's 2022 for goodness' sake and people still have a hard time accepting a woman in the pulpit! *How just how?! Do they forget about all the Biblical heroines? Do they just glance over those passages?* Because I know people will be people, I avoid opening that can of worms. Tactfully, I shift my attention to his siblings who are also ballbusters, but at least they're comical. *That reminds me I need to call my CoCo.* By the time Luke and I head out, his family loves me, but of course they do. *Why am I so loveable? Gosh, I'm such a treat and clearly so humble about it.* As we pull out of the driveway, the vibe changes slightly. *It just got really real, real quick.* He's serious. He wants to make plans, but I have a pending life-changing event so making long-term plans isn't quite the move right now, or honestly indefinitely. I'll just play it cool, and it'll be all good.

After cryptic responses, he finally gives up for the moment at least. As we say our goodnights, I am relieved. I go in and begin my nightly routine and prepare my mind for the morning. When I finally lay down in my cozy bed, I try to let the concerns of the day drift away and allow my eyes to close.

I refocus and get back to paperwork, but then my cell rings. Rosalind Ferrell is calling me and time stands still for a moment. A million thoughts go through my mind in a millisecond as if I'm Barry Allen speeding so fast that time seems eerily, silently still. This is the call that I've been waiting on for what seems like a lifetime. My heart is pounding out of my chest. All of the vetting is done. All of my reviews are in, and the deliberation process has ended. She's calling with the answer. The end-all, be-all of this act is on the other end of this call. I just have to answer it. This is one time that I absolutely do not want to hear the news over my voicemail. But what if the answer is no? What if she breaks my semblance of a heart? I'm at the office. No one sees the boss emotional. *Shucks, I barely see me emotional. I take a deep breath and answer the phone.*

"Hello Ms. Ferrell."

"Ms. Braxton, how are you?" *Not the pleasantries!*

"Well, and yourself?" She can hear the anxiety, I'm sure of it.

"Good, thank you. I have news for you."

"It's good I hope."

"I am happy to be the first to tell you that you have been approved. You are now a licensed foster parent and are officially able to adopt. You can begin looking for your child."

"Oh my goodness! Thank Jesus and thank you so much! I don't know what to say!"

"The official documents are already in the mail, but I wanted the pleasure of telling you first. Go celebrate, Ms. Braxton. Congratulations! I'll be in touch to schedule your first matching visit."

...

My parents are still in Phoenix, so I keep the news to myself until I get home to video call them. I don't know what to do! Things are finally falling into place. I'm going to be a mommy! *Me, a mommy! Finally!* They knew my situation and I was still approved. *Lord, I pray that I don't ruin this child's life. I haven't met her yet and I love her already.*

After sharing the news with Nita and Walt, I got a burst of energy that was the boost I needed to finish the work I had planned for the day. She, whoever she is, gave me the extra boost because it'll soon be official that I'm not just working for myself, but for my family. When I shut down my desktop at the office, I take some deep breaths to steady myself and head out for the day. I shut my business cell off early and decided to take a drive downtown by the water before going home.

Pulling up to the house, the excitement and gratitude overshadow the discomfort my body is in. Once I walk in the house, I set the alarm, close all the blinds and leave on the night lights because I can feel I won't make it back down here tonight. I'm too tired to force myself to eat, so I go shower and get in the bed.

When I awake, something is wrong. It's 3:47 am and I'm panting for air. Typically, I wouldn't be alarmed, but I can't catch my breath and the shooting pain in my back and legs are out of the norm. I just took two treatments with no relief. I hear my father's voice in my head, so I make myself get presentable enough to take myself to the hospital. Much to my surprise, when I get there I'm nearly immediately admitted. It's the whole circus of tests and all those shenanigans of IVs with fluids attached to me. I've been poked and probed all morning and I'm not here for it. If they allow me a moment of no disturbance to collect myself and close my eyes for a minute, I'll call Meaghan and have her hold all my conference calls and whatever meetings I left on the books. It looks like I'll be here at least for a day. When Meaghan shows up after I told her it was unnecessary, she tells me that Luke showed up at the office. *I legit wanna know who gave this nigga drop-by privileges! I let that junk slide once or twice, but this is too much.* And yep, his call is right on time.

"Why didn't you tell me you were sick?" *This nigga got a lil too much bass in his voice right now.*

"Because telling you wouldn't have made me feel better." *Was that rude? I typically don't know until after it flies out my mouth. This. This is why niggas don't like me.*

At this very moment, it sinks in that I can no longer let Luke linger. He's looking for a wife, and frankly I ain't her, at least not for him. He's great and has no huge deal-breaker character flaws, except for the fact that he isn't it for me. He's mentioned quite often about my lack of public displays of affection or really any displays of affection towards him. Aside from the fact that I don't need to be playing with fire, I still have to prepare myself for his touch. I still tolerate it as opposed to wanting it. When we kick it it's cool and enjoyable, but I'm still ready for the night to end. I never actually miss him nor ache for his very presence. At times, when I'm bored I may think "oh what is he doing," but I can't honestly say I make an effort to make time for him. When something major occurs, good or bad, I don't have the immediate urge to call him. I don't like wasted time and I don't want to waste his time either.

That wouldn't be fair to him. But now is probably
not the right time though... I should want him
here. Telling him should make me feel better
because I know he'd do whatever he could for me.
I want to miss someone even when it aches. I
want it to be natural to want to be touched by
someone and share all my affection with that
someone. I want to automatically reach out to
someone when something big happens. I guess, if
I really thought Luke was the one, I would've told
him about the adoption and been more
transparent with my health and the vulnerability
it forces. I really did want to like him.

Control Freak

I am trying to find peace in between the beeps of all the machinery attached to me. When it's silent my thoughts are the loudest, so much so that I can't even hear myself think straight. Reality hits me. Though over a decade now, I still remember when I couldn't control my own body. I remember many of the nasty things people said about me and some even had the gall to say it to me directly. That's probably on the list of reasons why I keep things like this private. I remember being pulled out of driver's training around my 16th birthday because it was too dangerous for me to drive. I remember not knowing what would happen, so I exercised as much control as possible. I control what people see and how much of it. Ironically, I'm fully aware that I'm not in ultimate control over my own being, but I have the closest thing to that, a relationship with the only One who does. No matter what happens in my life, He holds me in His hand and there is great assurance in that. Even with my current status, it brings me comfort. The gift of motherhood I didn't give to myself. I couldn't control that, and I'm all the more grateful. Peace that surpasses all understanding is what He gives.

This sentiment gets me to the point where I can close my eyes and drift to sleep until the nurse comes probing again. *I gotta bust up outta here.*

Knowing all of this, I am still human. The urge to control my own destiny still pulls at me.

Being chronically ill with something unknown is already a feat, but you add in sheer incompetence, lack of bedside manner, and systemic racism and you get a big cup of hell naw. As a teenager, before that temptation was even a real thing for me, I was accused of being pregnant when I had tremors. Because I was young and most importantly Black I had to have been lying about being a virgin and couldn't have possibly been afraid of being afflicted by a faceless giant that ravaged my body and left me with little to zero control of my own person. I had to be dramatic. Because I was a Black teen, I had to have been drinking. The folks who opened their mouths to say I was attention-seeking would change their story if they knew the hell I went through not just with the physical battle, but the battle with so-called professionals. I had to begin getting answers on my own. The physical struggles changed then multiplied, but the relentless experience of being a Black woman in America needing medical help surely grew more gruesome over the years. The things that I have experienced and witnessed, even with Black professionals, would astound some people. For this reason, I am a firm believer in self-advocacy and advocating for the village. I pay attention to my care. I'm not a doctor, but I seek clarity and sound advice, especially in dealing with my health. I try to be proactive and encourage others to do the same. One of the main things I have the honor of speaking to young people about is advocacy. I have the responsibility of stewardship and being able to take my medical team seriously is a part of that.

...

After a couple days, I'm back to my normal and decide to ease back into the rhythm. I hop in the Lincoln and head to the café. I exchange pleasantries with regulars and work the room just for a minute. I missed being here. It feels like home, sometimes more than my own home. After I wrap up a few conversations, I go get down to business. Monday is our early day, so I go grab Chel and Sam to discuss a hiccup. Unfortunately, I have to terminate a contract with a supplier because he's in breach. The farmer was organic local and had some scruples, but he is no longer even compliant with the piss poor low codes that the law requires. After having to throw the whole farm away and begin looking for another, I am beat. I return to the whip, cruising home in the classic I play "Slap" by Luda then transition to "Mr. Nigga" by Mos Def. I guess it's just one of those days.

When I get home to unwind, I respond to some personal texts. I leave Luke on unread because I still haven't had the heart to drop him, so I resort to 'The Nanny' reruns and wind down. I doze off and my eyes open around 2:35 am. Before trying to get back to sleep, I get in my Word. It brings me right back to my control revelries. Colossians 1:17 and Jeremiah 29:11 really hit me. I apparently have some work to do *or rather work at doing less sometimes.* Man, it is something about when the Word convicts you. There's no way to ignore that. As I take in this revelation, I close my eyes and hope to sleep peacefully.

...

I'm battling to keep my eyes open. I think I went a little too hard with Mr. Everlast this morning. This meeting was supposed to be 30 minutes or less and now it's been over an hour. I guess it's my fault. Maybe if I spent more time at Dope I wouldn't have this problem. I know my graphics team is tired of me, but we have to get this right. My gifting simply isn't in executing the visual art, but certain things I see very vividly, so I rely heavily on descriptions. Here's this control again...

As this is getting beyond tedious, I give the team a break and my mind drifts. I'm about to be somebody's mom. *That's wild. I can't fully describe what I'm experiencing. I think it's wonder and excitement with a tinge of weight and fear.* My thoughts were quickly interrupted as the team came back and gave me exactly what I was waiting for, and it was brilliant. The new line for the pop-up series is about to be poppin'!

When I hop in the Lincoln, my phone buzzes and it's Grey. Somehow I've agreed to lunch. I guess I could use a break. That meeting was brutal, but then it ended on a glorious note. Plus, I can use him as my unusual voice of reason.

"So are you still with ole boy?"

"Well, just dive right in don't ya"

"Well, are you?"

"Nah, but he don't know that yet. I tried."

"So what was the problem with this one?"

"If you must know, he just wasn't it. He was cool. He's kind and caring and all that, but you know me. It's either there or it ain't. I never got used to him being around. I was never completely comfortable around him and he's looking for a wife. I'm not ready for that. Well, not for him. I guess that's the nutshell version of it."

"So you're not ready to be a wife, but you're ready to be a mom?"

"Ah, down to the nitty gritty I see! Mmm, well Grey, you were apparently ready to be a father before being a husband too."

"Touché! You got me there."

"Of course I did. I won. Plus, I don't have a baby daddy so it's different. If I was becoming a mom the old-fashioned way at this time, the goal would absolutely be to be a wife first, but that's just not what it is right now, not to say that it won't be one day."

"I see."

"How is the mini you by the way? He really is adorable."

"Thank you and he's doing really well. Still growing and teaching me something new every day."

"I was approved. I am going on a visit this week to start looking for my daughter."

"You serious?!"

"Yes, and I can tell no one else, but I'm a nervous wreck. It's crazy. I'm excited but it's weird. I don't know how to look for a kid. It's not like going shopping for shoes."

"Just breathe. You'll be great. You take care of everyone you can and you'll be the best mom to that little girl, whoever she is." *Welp, I guess this wasn't a waste after all.*

"Your faith in me is uncanny."

After catching up well into the evening, we go our separate ways. *This wasn't as awkward as I thought it would be.*

...

At the visit, I'm mid sentence with Rosalind and am stopped in my tracks. I see her. I see my daughter. She's beautiful. She has cocoa brown skin and she has the brightest, deepest brown eyes. They're special. They're etched into my soul. They look like they've seen a lot, but are still full of hope. I see her. I'm looking at my child. I did not know what to expect and I nearly bolted out of the door, but I steadied my breath and excused myself. I headed to the restroom to calm myself a bit.

All of the waiting and anticipation has come to this moment and I see her, but I don't know if she sees me. *What if she doesn't want me as a mom? What if I am too...well, too me for her?* All of the elements outside of my control come crashing down and only hope keeps me from panicking. It's a good thing I wore makeup today on account of the extra luggage under my eyes because Lord knows half my life just exited and re entered my face in two point two seconds.

I hurriedly strut out of the restroom and resume my stroll with Rosalind. *Let's do this.* Though approved, the process of actually taking the kid home varies, so I want to pace myself, *BUT I SAW HER! SHE IS LITERALLY RIGHT THERE WAITING ON ME TO LEARN HOW TO BE HER MOMMY, BUT SHE PROBABLY DOESN'T EVEN KNOW IT YET! Breathe Kenny, breathe.* When we settle in the meeting area, I ask to speak to that little girl. She's alone, but I don't perceive her to be shy. She looks about eight or nine. I try to keep my cool so I don't scare the kid. I think I'm doing a good job.

…

Sitting high in the truck, I am carried away; I was going to the café but everything is under control and nothing else requires my attention at the complex, so somehow I end up at my comfort food spot. I think two of my favorite things are befitting after meeting the kid I believe to be my kid.

I am having what my mom would call a "stolen moment." Whenever she sparsely had a moment to herself during her tenure of caring for her mother, those moments were definitely stolen in the eyes of Granny. It's funny, as I grow closer to becoming a parent, I am more introspective of my own parents and their choices in raising me.

I'm not sure if my parents ever got to live out their dreams. I don't find that fair. I'm certain that they both worked hard to give my sister and me a chance to live ours. A part of me grieves for their loss, though I'm fully aware that every opportunity costs. Langston Hughes never lied when he proclaimed, "life ain't been no crystal stair, but I'm extremely grateful for every sacrifice they made. Every brick of the home I built was laid because of them. My companies exist because of them. I hate the term "self-made" because the Lord made me, gave me ability, and honored my obedience to Him. That's why I'm on the path I'm on, I'm seeking His glory. But in the societal sense, I'm seen as a self-made, first generation entrepreneur, owning 100% of my corporation, but I could only build on the foundation Walt & Nita laid in my life. My dreams include a family of my own, a family to leave a spiritual and natural legacy. I pray that I'm not projecting too much of my dreams onto my soon-to-be child already. I pray that I continue to seek fulfillment holistically. I know that having a kid will come with challenges, but I'd like to think none of them are regrettable. I often pray that I haven't been too burdensome to my own parents.

When I get home, I sit in my oversized truck looking at this big ole house thinking about when

I'll make it a home for that gorgeous little girl when I am interrupted by a pressing matter. Luke is calling, and I cannot ignore this any longer. *Well, I could do like my alleged nigga nature and simply ignore him forever and then a year later pretend like we amicably went our separate ways, but I've been told that's not nice and apparently not ladylike. Who knew?*

"Hello"

"So she lives…" His voice makes it known the levels to his emotions.

"Yes, I live. I've just had a lot going on."

"I take it you're not busy now. Are you home? I'm in the area, do you mind if I swing by?" Silence is loud. M*eeting his family was definitely a bad idea… For that, I am sorry.*

Before I know it, "Ok" escapes my mouth.

Hanging up my phone, I jump down from the Ram and head into the house. It's a shame. *I'm so* short. I have a step and STILL have to jump. Well, God didn't want to give me too much sauce I suppose.

Not shortly after unlocking the door and resetting the alarm, Luke pulls up to the house. To my surprise he skips many of the pleasantries. Upon letting him in, he decides that he would like to go to some scenic place to have a conversation and go on an impromptu date, no doubt it'll be about "our future."

"You don't have anything else to do, let's go." *First of all, did this nigga just say that out his mouth?!*

"James, I'm not even gone address that statement, but I do need to tell you what's been on my mind and why I have not been so responsive. Getting to know you these past months has been nice, and you are such a wonderful man, but I don't think this is going to work. A part of me wishes it would, but I don't want to waste anymore of our time."

"So just like that? You met my people and led me on for months for nothing."

"It was not my intention to lead you on, and truthfully it was too late to cancel meetin' yo fam."

"Wow."

"I truly believe that you'll be a fantastic husband; I just don't believe you are mine and it wouldn't be fair to keep dangling." *I tried. I thought I was into him or at least on my way there, but then I got that wonderful news.*

"Don't tell me you gone hit me wit the 'let's be friends.'"

"I wasn't, but I can leave cordial acquaintances on the table." *This is why I don't get involved with clients…*

"I see."

"I hope you don't end up hating me. I tried. I hope this doesn't end our business relationship, but if it does, I understand."

"No, not at all. Your firm's work has increased productivity already and I can separate your business entity from you."

"Okay. I am really sorry."

"Don't apologize for telling the truth. Maybe with better timing, there would be a different outcome." *I doubt it dawg, but I'll let you have it. And for the record, I ain't apologizing for the truth, I'm sorry because behind his ego I can sense he's hurt and I avoided confrontation.*

"Maybe so."

"I got to be honest though, too. I was beginning to fall for you."

"Nah, maybe not me, maybe the idea of me." *You didn't truly know me.*

He had no idea of my quirks or how I function. He knew more than most, but not enough for something real. I guess that was my fault. *Okay fine, it was my fault, absolutely my fault.* He has no idea of who I am and how most days I make no sense while making perfect sense. He doesn't know, and I don't have the time nor the desire to let him. This I can control.

The goal is not to make niggas sick after things don't work out, and in this case it's not like Luke's done anything wrong. I just know myself well enough to know this ain't it. The goal also isn't to get someone better than him. If the love sung about in 90s R&B happens for me, the goal is to get someone better for me, someone I complement and vice versa. Someone not perfect, but perfect for me-as cliché as that sounds. If it happens, I'll know. I just believe when you know you know.

I woke up with more ferocity than normal. Today instead of a sheep, I am a lioness.

After my morning session with Mr. Everlast, I got myself together for the day. One of the critical roles of an entrepreneur is finding a diplomatic way to say, "run me my money." This is a client's third time in the last six months missing a payment, and that's not how this works. I have employees to pay and benefit packages to fund. I ain't got time for tardy payments. Money isn't at the top of the list, but it is most definitely on the list of things I don't play about. *If it ain't off da love, it's likely on the money.* These leopard print stilettos and I have a job to do today. As I stride to the Challenger with its tank sitting on full, I'm thrown back to a moment in time.

...

A few years back my gas light came on. To me this was rock bottom, *so I thought.* At that point, I felt like a whole bum. I'm certain my survival skills would have gotten me through if I didn't live with my parents because they equipped me, but I was most definitely in a tight spot. Looking at that empty gas tank, I thought about all the people who owed me money. Of course, I knew I wasn't going to get it back when I gave it, and Daddy taught me not to give what I needed. I also learned that lesson the hard way once or twice. I held onto that principle, but clearly didn't think everything through all the time. *The should've, could've, would've was on my mind....* I was pissed it was too late to return merchandise waiting to go to print. Dope was still coming straight out of my pocket, so it was at a standstill until a miracle was to come. My friends I introduced were going out together without me because I not only was sick, I was broke. I hated asking for money and nearly cried in my car. I was dreading going in the house waiting for Walt to wake up and get ready for work so I could ask for gas money to get to class. I can still hear the cuss out for even allowing my tank to get so low when I don't normally. *I'm not the I-know-my-tank kinda chick.* With all my accounts on empty and one overdrawn, I was tapped out. He didn't know that I had to be Godmom-Save-A-Kid , or GG as Ivy called me, the night before. Flying like a bat out of hell is not good for the tank, but I had to save her. There was a shooting downtown near her school where she performed that night. I was there earlier to support her, but left when she assured me she had a ride. When I got that call and heard how shaken she was knowing she was alone, I would've ran barefoot if I had to. She was stranded and shook up. I had to do what I had to do. *Somebody did!*

All types of realities were coming down on me and it only took a gas light to illuminate them. I was broke. *Never a broke hoe though.* I was facing an even more prolonged graduation because financial aid was praying on my downfall. This was truly an insult to injury because I'd been bargaining with God all semester just about staying healthy enough to finish. I suppose I forgot to pray about the financial part, or maybe I just wasn't praying fervently enough. I just couldn't seem to catch a break. To say I was dependent was an understatement, and I hated it! I was grateful, but conflicted. My mom still paid my car insurance. My dad bailed me out the previous summer so I could enroll in that semester, so how could I ask him again? The thought of crawling back to my dad for help was mortifying. College wasn't even a choice growing up with my parents. Where was I gone go right out of high school? My health was uncertain, so I needed more help than I'd even wanted to ask for at the time. I struggled through school for missing so many classes due to flares and specialist appointments, when I didn't want to go in the first place. *I still got them loans looking at me in my face right now, too.* Nita went to most of my appointments with me at the time, and she and Walt were footing the bill for most, if not all the meds I was taking. It seemed to all come back down to my body, so I ended up in a place I loathe. I landed in a "if I wasn't sick I wouldn't be in this place" place. *That place.* That was truly rock bottom.

That gas light exacerbated my desperation and fury. I began putting in job apps, convinced I'd just grind my final semester. I was getting rejection letters from jobs I was overqualified for and new clients for Black Out were nowhere to be found because it was our dry season. I was stuck. I was livid. I was sitting in my car with an empty tank coming home from church. *Where could I go from there?*

I had to stop having a pity party and remember who I was. I had to get back focused because quite frankly I was pissing myself off. I had to look my situation in the face and say "eff you." I knew that being sick was not going to be my excuse for living with my parents forever or the convenient excuse for quitting jobs with terrible management, so I got my game face on. I was not playing. That gas light, the rock bottom, that pity all had to go. God had already shown me too much for me to turn back, so I had a choice to make. Be a punk or boss up. After I was humbled, I bossed up.

...

Throughout this whole meeting Johnny Pay Lately stutters and trips over his own words. He can tell I didn't come to play with him. I am a relatively understanding person, but there seems to be no valid reason for the constant late payments and, as per our contract, the longer it remains outstanding the more the penalties increase. This man just bought new expensive and quite tasteless furnishings for his office. *Can we say oooglay.* He also has a Ferrari parked in the lot. *How ostentatious of him....* If you can rent a Ferrari, you can afford to pay Black Out's invoice on time. If he wants to play with me and cancel this contract before term, he has to pay to dissolve it. I doubt he'll want to do something that crazy, my team has his business running efficiently and their client base has increased substantially since they've contracted with us, so that would be a gigantic loss for him. *I don't have these problems with my Black excellence clients.* Truthfully, it took me a long time to accept white clients. *No, I'm not a racist. Militant maybe, but not a racist.* My culture is ingrained in all my work, and unfortunately, I have experienced great opposition as a Black woman in business. I paid all the costs, so I have a right and reason to be selective in accepting clientele. A lot of white folks are still benefiting off wealth amassed from the oppression of my people. That's not necessarily their fault, at least not always. The sins of the father are not of the son, but my issue is that many act like they don't know. They compare themselves to folks who look like me who never owned land when we're still recovering from red lined districts, Jim Crow laws, remnants of slavery that have yet to be abolished, etc. They get to own land that slaves were beaten on while they worked dawn till nightfall. Most times when we start something it is from scratch because we were left with nothing. We were stolen from whatever home we knew and for generations we have been here, much of what we built here has been violently ravaged, and no DNA test can refute the fact that connections were lost. They get to talk about the Mayflower and how their ancestors were brave coming across the ocean whereas my people didn't have a choice. Shoot even some of our own sold us out to salvage what they could of their own. All of this history goes into my businesses and with whom I work with because I make it a point to stand united with my culture and build up community, not just business. *That doesn't mean I promote what's wrong just because the people doing it look like me either.* I treat my employees with respect, dignity, and grace because we do not always get even half of that outside our own, but I do hold great yet realistic expectations of my team. That's why people run me money because I've earned it. I built this corporation from the ground up with George Shunger in the back of my mind rooting for me to succeed for my village and the support of my family.

As I leave his office with the completed payment and hop into the Challenger, I try to keep my militant thoughts at bay when my phone rings.

"This is Braxton."

"Hey girl! How you been?" This voice is vaguely familiar, but not easily recognizable. Why did I answer? I keep mixing up my personal cell with my business cell.

"I'm smooth, but I'm sorry who is this? How did you get my personal number?"

"It's me, Janet. You were just on my mind and I wanted to hit you up. I haven't talked to you in a while." *Janet? Ohhhh, Janet from undergrad.* She's one of those whom I was a friend to, but she didn't quite make the cut as my friend. She only hits me up when she wants something. *Today is not the day to want something from me.*

"That's nice of you. I'm handling some business right now though, can I hit you back?"

"Yes, of course, but I just want you to think about something. I know you invest and wanted to know if you'd invest in my startup." *Of course, money is what she wants!*

"Contact Braxton Holdings Inc. There's a form on the website or you can call the office to speak to one of the receptionists for more info.

Someone from my office will get some info from you and if you seem like a probable candidate, a rep will send you a formal application and begin the process."

"So formal. Don't you just want to help out a friend?" *She clearly uses that term loosely.*

"As you used the term invest, I'm sure you want real money. You forget I got a business degree and sense. Heavy on the sense! This ain't spotting you a twenty here and there like in college. If I was a lesser woman, I would've had a running tab and invoiced you back then, but I'm a cool chick. When real money is involved, paperwork is involved. I personally don't just invest all willy nilly. My corporation invests. Am I in charge of that? Yes, but there are people and procedures I have in place."

"Dang, it's like that? You think you all that now and too good to help yo girl?"

"Cut the crap. I haven't heard from you in I don't even know. You typically only get in touch when you want something, and though giving is a beautiful gift, I am not obligated to give every time you come with your hand out. My girl? Girl bye. You know good and well we're acquaintances at best. I wish you the best in your endeavors. Don't call my phone with this foolishness again." *CLICK! Man, I miss the old flip*

Despite the image I portray, I have a hard time saying no and I have a terrible habit of apologizing entirely too much. Learning how to refrain from saying sorry for not allowing someone to take advantage of me changed my life, and today is one of those days. I'm done apologizing for what's out of my control or for even doing what I feel like doing or not doing at the moment. Niggas love calling me when they want something from me, but today I'm choosing to say no to favors. Today I'm off. As much as I work for Black excellence and community, I don't have time for leeches. They are the Achilles' heel of the community. Yes, we were oppressed. Yes, things are not fair, but we cannot live everyday using the obvious as an excuse. We are either gone do or not. We all need help sometimes, but that's not this.

Shaking off her phone call, "Party Up (Up In Here)" by DMX comes on and the timing is rich. Pushing to the complex to make my rounds in the offices. I decided to take a short day, since I'll be in the café for the rest of the week.

After making my rounds, I realize I didn't cut the day that short, but getting home at 7pm isn't so bad given when I started. When I pull up to my house, I see way too many cars. Dang! I forgot

Daddy was having his football club meeting here tonight. My parents are renovating their house and the mini house can be a bit crowded. I don't mind when they entertain people here, but I'm really not in the mood to deal with a whole lot of humans. Now, I have to wear real clothes if I want to be downstairs until they're gone. *At least I have a mini fridge in my room. It's for emergencies, but this is an emergency. I need to be alone immediately.*

As soon as I get in the door, one of the football clubbers makes eye contact. *Gosh darnit! Be invisible. Be invisible right now!*

"Hey _______, how you doing?" *No, he did not just call me that out his mouth through his lips!*

"Only my dad can call me that. And I'm fine, thank you. How are you?"

"Lil girl I'm a grown a** man. I've known you since you were in diapers. I'll call you what I want." *This nigga must be drunk and crazy. Which side he got me effed up on, over here or over there?*

"You are a grown man. And yeah you may have seen me at a few functions a year since I was in diapers, but you have never changed one. You don't know me like that and haven't had one hand in my upbringing, and if you haven't noticed I'm a grown woman. You are in MY house so it would behoove you to act like it and show some respect." He looks at me with shock and does not say a word. *Yeah, that's right I'm not one of those docile women who you run all over. Got me fifty shades of messed up in my house. I will fight you, sir! I got time today! Ooooh he betta be glad my daddy just walked over here.*

"Hey baby girl, everything alright?" *Yeah, once I smack yo mans.*

"Yeah Daddy, everything is alright with me. Are we clear now, everything aight?"

"Yeah, young lady everything is good." *Talkin' to me crazy in MY house. I paid the cost to be the boss up in this mug gotdangit!*

I have a baseline of respect for every human being. The Lord is still working on me with some, but I was raised to respect my elders even more so because they've experienced what I've never seen. Walt did however tell me that just because someone is older than me doesn't mean I owe them respect, meaning if they had me messed up, I didn't have to accept it. I took that and ran with it. *So what folks not gone do is talk to me stupid. Homeboy was getting kicked smoove out. Why are people trying me today? Maybe I just need to sleep.*

I just don't get it. On my way home, I had to turn up on some miscreant at the gas station. I was getting below a half tank and decided to just fill up since it was still light out. Most days I ignore the tomfoolery, but today was just not the day to sit on my whip, assume it's my man's and then try to turn around to spit some whack game. *Well, maybe I didn't have to turn up on him... I've been secretly wishing a nigga would all day.* I really have to get it together. Ephesians 4:26 "Be ye angry but sin not; don't let the sun go down on your wrath" flashed in my brain. *Okay God you right!* I haven't been talking to the Lord and in my Word as much as I should the last couple of days. That's why I've been on tip. I need to go talk to Jesus.

My father once told me that he wasn't a nice man for a time. The crazy thing is I'm his child. I ain't been good to every person who crossed my path. I ain't a hero in every story. Admittedly, I've been the villain more than I even know. There are probably some folks who don't like me for good reason. Everybody ain't lying. *I mean, most probably are, but everybody ain't. Some accusations are valid.* I can't go back and erase anything. All I can do is try to be a better human than I was before. It doesn't mean I'm not remorseful. It means I won't choose the cycle of reliving the past when I can live right now. Nor will I pretend that wanting a reason to turn up on somebody is okay. Some Christians pretend like they never did wrong or as if anything they did before is just washed away without us asking for forgiveness and acknowledging our mess. I might not ever see those folks I done wrong again, even if it was just saying the wrong thing at the wrong time, be it maliciously or not. That gets me a lot, but even when I can't make amends with them, I can still pray for them, repent, and keep it pushing. Though I was seemingly justified, I was in my flesh today *and that's never where it's at...* I work every day to be decent and kind. I work hard to root myself in Christ to be the righteousness of God because I alone am not a very nice woman, if nice at all.

Sometimes at night when I can't sleep and don't feel like cooking, I walk around this big house and pray, just meditate and try to reel in my thoughts. Looking around, people would say I've done well for myself or talk about what I've done. *Shucks, sometimes I say it too, but it's not me who did all this. I didn't give myself any ability.* Every now and then I think of how much further I'd be if I didn't have so many constraints. I just imagine where I'd be if I was completely healthy. In my mind I'd be legit poppin', but even if I was who's to say I'd be that beast I think I would be? Plus, if I was, I'd likely be a mean cuss word to say the least. I'm right where God wants me to be. I get out of hand enough as it is now. The constraints make up the thorn in my side. It serves its purpose to bring God glory in unfathomable ways and to keep me humble. Even if no one else knows it, I know that God makes it possible for me to get up and go as hard as I do, to be the Don in Heels, to be the lioness unleashed, and to get money not let money have me. "His grace is sufficient…"

The Death of Dysfunction

I'm finally back in bed. It's taking me a minute to get to sleep. I'm in a twilight. I feel myself having chills and sweats. Suddenly, I am 12 years old again. I'm in a dark place, but then the lights come on. Danielle, Mama, and I are positioned in a triangle. I see us at the old house packing up some things, namely George Shunger's guns to take home to Daddy. I'm standing at an end table going through the drawer. I see shells, but Ma gets my attention by calling my name in that southern accent of hers. *The woman lived in Detroit for over 50 some odd years and still sounded like she was from the backwoods of Alabama. George Shunger always said she was from "dem sticks wit her sticky a**."*

I look up and I am staring down the barrel of a pistol. I don't know what my 12-year-old self is thinking. I'm frozen in time. 12-year-old me is probably wondering "is she really gone shoot a nigga." Her finger was on the trigger. She had a stroke. Her hands were unsteady. Knowing my grandfather, that gun was very likely loaded. I wonder what would've happened if that gun did go boom. Out of nowhere, it's like fast-forward was hit. I'm 20 or so, lying down and talking to Mommy. I tell her. No one other than Danielle knows, and even she forgot. At this time, Mama is either on her deathbed or already gone. I don't truly know my rhyme or reason, but as this resurfaces my mind nearly a decade later, I have a few educated guesses. I suppose I didn't tell because my folks were on rocky ground. Around that time my mom moved out of the house. My parents were separated on the brink of divorce again. Nita would've believed me, but Walt wouldn't have, or he would've chalked it up to her playing or having had a stroke. I grew up around guns, but I was taught about them. I was first taught that it wasn't a toy, so I knew when my grandma pulled a gun on me that she likely was not just *playing*. I mean, when she said that the Lord didn't care about my soul, it was a joke. *It was evil as hell, but it was apparently a joke.* Her voice and comedic timing made people laugh. I can justify some things for the sake of her jokes. Shucks, I can laugh at some of them too, but I don't see how staring at me point blank with a gun directly aimed at me is comical in any way. If there ever was a reason she did that I'll never know now.

I'm back in my current time, but I cannot will myself to wake up even though the sweats are drenching me entirely. Why did this come to mind? *Why would she do that?* Clearly, I never asked her about it. I didn't remember until she was dying. A year or two after I told my mom, it came up in conversation with Danielle as we were talking about Mama. She tried to argue me down; she said, "All I remember is ducking and you standing there looking all hard like 'really Ma' then-"

"How funny, you ducking while it's pointed at me," I interjected.

"Mama didn't point it at you. She waved it around and then pointed it at you." *Sometimes I think she is a female Trucky from Pootie Tang fareal.*

"Exactly, she pointed it at me! Her aim was in my direction."

"Ken, you know what? Mama did do you the dirtiest out of all of us."

What's ironic is that we laughed about this, though there's no actual humor. None of that was okay at all. Not a single piece of it. I still can't get over her unsteady finger resting on that trigger. *It could have gone off...Why didn't it go off? I wonder if she was upset that it didn't.* I suppose it could have been categorized as a traumatic experience. I don't feel traumatized. *I mean having a dream about it fifteen years later causing sweats and chills probably isn't normal, but oh well. It's just a bad dream. YOU CAN WAKE UP AT ANYTIME NOW!!* One time Danielle had the audacity to say, "you need to see a therapist and get over it." I literally almost punched her in the throat. I wasn't so much as affected by it as I was baffled, plus that's easy for someone to say when apparently that "sweet old lady" didn't quite do her the worst. Was it that episode mixed with the weight of loss that caused my body to despise itself so much that it attacks itself? Well, when I grieved or dealt with this supposed trauma wouldn't the health problems just go away if trauma is what brought it? I've never had my money on this hypothesis, so I never truly sought out the help I probably desperately needed at the time. After that lady asked me if I prayed to saints when I was forced to go to therapy after the earthquakes ravaged my body in high school, I never had it in me to speak with one even though I knew therapists and people who sought out help. I vehemently encouraged people to seek help and to be unashamed, yet here I am always determined to handle it all on my own. I'm still taken aback by the prevalence of dysfunction, but really the issue is pretending it does not exist. The concept is the same with evil in the world. The problem that we have is pretending that there is no existence of evil as opposed to resisting it, correcting it even. I preached on that not too long ago. Funny how sermons preached always hit the preacher.

...

Finally, my eyes are open. I'm not even mad that it's 4am. As I'm soaking wet from sweat and still battling chills, I decide to take a bath. Maybe it'll be more soothing at this time of stillness. Sitting in the tub, I try to self-sooth. I sing in hopes of consoling myself. Not before long, I'm over this bath, though it was nice while it lasted. I shower and head to the guest room because I'm in no mood to change my linen. I'll deal with that tomorrow. I lay down and my mind drifts. I say a prayer and close my eyes.

I stay in bed until 10am. The good thing about being the boss is that you can work from home sometimes, but the bad thing about working from home is being distracted by household responsibilities. Stuff that's supposed to shine is getting dusty, I still have to change my linen that got drenched in sweat, and I need to take inventory of my pantry.

Oh, thank God! The cleaning crew comes in this week for their day this month. I clean up after myself, but this is a big ole house and I'm just one person whose mind apparently just does not know how to stop. I have three conference calls, then I need to take a look at the books. I have an accountant, but ya girl don't play that. People going to jail in these streets or going belly up because they didn't keep track of what their paid accountants did. *Chile please.* Darn, I also have some plan development to do. I check up on my business plans every so often to see if I'm on target to reach goals, but more importantly sticking to the mission and vision. I also like to fine tune it when needed in case we qualify for funding. *Ain't neva too big to stop getting other people's money the right way.* I also need to schedule a meeting with my team to discuss who Braxton Holdings is investing in next. *I know who it won't be…if ole girl actually applied.* I just want a nap. I remember the days when if I missed plan development, it would be okay. Because I did Dope and Black Out backwards I was always catching up trying to finish the business plans after they were already operational. Of course I was frustrated, but it wasn't as big of a deal. I have too many people attached to me to not do what I have to do. Speaking of, I need to finish preparing for the staff meetings at all entities tomorrow. I'll be at the complex all day.

Another day has gone by in a flash. As I'm winding down for the day, I did everything on my work to-do list, but I still haven't changed my linen, which is a must. All the beds are clearly mine, but I want MY bed. I need to do laundry anyway. There's a blouse I want to wear to match my shoes for tomorrow. Welp I better pop on an attention-grabbing show or I'll be asleep on this couch with my favorite throw blanket. I would start Game of Thrones again, but I don't want to pay that much attention.

I should probably call the doctor. I'm still having chills and come to think of it, I've been having them for a few days. I just feel sick. Most days it feels like I'm fighting something, but when it lingers I typically know it's another infection. I don't always seek treatment, but my remedies don't seem to be cutting it and this can't get out of hand since I'm busy the next two weeks or so. Thankfully doubling up on vitamins and natural remedies isn't a big ordeal for me when it's seldom done. My body can balance itself back out, *but them drugs on the other hand...* It's funny how the mind and body work together. I thought those chills were just due to that dream. I've noticed that sometimes nightmares wake me up because something may be wrong physically or they could very well just be a bad dream that may or may not be shining a light on the dysfunction to which we've become accustomed.

While I wait for the buzzer to go off to tell me that my sheets are dry, I think of my daughter. I get to go back for a visit in two days. The thought of bringing her home is a pleasant change from my earlier revelries. It's only 10pm so I call Mom before she goes to bed.

"Hey baby cakes."

"Hey girl hey. How are you?"

"I'm okay. How are you? I miss ya. I ain't heard from you all day."

"I'm okay girlfriend, and I know Mommy. It's been a long day, but I'll bring dinner over and hang out with you and Daddy on Wednesday. I'll come after Bible study."

"Ooh you know we ain't had lamb chops in a while or grilled salmon and we need some Key Lime Pie."

"You don't know what you want," I can't help but laugh at this lady.

"You know I like snacks. You're the mommy of the cooking"

"Ha! Well, Momma speaking of me being the mommy, I saw her. I saw my daughter when I went on my visit with Ms. Ferrell. She's beautiful and brilliant. I visit again on Wednesday afternoon."

I know she wanted to ask if I was ready again, but I'm in deep and she couldn't hide her excitement to be a grandma. I'm elated that my baby won't have to worry, she won't question whether or not her grandma loves her. My mom won't try to bribe her with nice things with ulterior motives to get one up on me. She won't criticize every single thing about her. She won't tell her that the Lord cares nothing about her soul and she'd never in a million years pull a gun out on her. She'll be okay. She'll be more than okay. She'll be loved beyond measure and the acceptance of dysfunction will stop at my door, *our door.*

As I climb the final stair with the basket of linen, I look at the room to be hers and imagine us going through catalogs to decorate it just how she likes it. I want this house to be her safe haven, her home. I want this room to be a representation of her. I know materials are just things, but we can use these things for representation. The problem is when things dictate the expression. I want her to be herself unapologetically. I want her to express herself in healthy ways. I know that boundaries will be important, especially since I did not have the privilege of birthing her. To her this will be a foreign place. I just pray I don't come on too strong when I see her again. *Dear Lord, I'm going to be somebody's momma.*

...

Ahh, there's nothing like just having showered and shaved and jumping into fresh linen. As I say my prayers and wind down, I ask the Lord to be able to sleep through the night and wake up rejuvenated, and of course I say a prayer of covering over her.

I'm wearing printed pumps with lilac, red, and yellow. Today I'm in the classic, the Lincoln, and I head to the complex. Instead of my normal rushing, I take my time. When I pull up to the complex, I go to the café because I had Michele make a few items for her sister teams. They always complain about how jealous they get since all the good stuff is down here, including me most of the time.

Meaghan accompanies me to all the meetings as my right hand. She's done all the agendas for me, which is perfect because I forgot. I begin with Dope, who just hired a new employee. Looking at the increase of sales, I can't help but thank Akilah. She holds Dope down for me. I normally am only super hands-on when our annual events are going on and when there is a problem, but she seldom needs me to put out fires. After the meetings are over, I call her to my office so I can give her a little gift.

"I know you thought I forgot your birthday is today."

"Is that what I think it is?"

"Open it and see."

"OH MY GOSH! IT IS!" She's been wanting a pair of these stilettos like the ones I'm wearing for so long.

"You deserve them and more. I also made the mandarin orange pineapple cake filled with whipped cream infused with rum and frosted in an orange German buttercream just like you like it."

"Kenny, thank you so much!"

"No, thank you. You have taken care of my first baby so well and I am forever grateful! Happiest Birthday, Girl!" I hand her the birthday card with her overdo raise in it.

Before I know it, she jumps up and hugs me. I'm not even mad, but this chick will not have me tear up.

Now, moving on down the line. Meaghan headed to Black Out before me to round up the troops, so when I got there, we jumped right in. Johnny-Pay-Lately seems to have gotten his act together, but a few other clients may need some act right as well. They're almost to term so I'll discuss with the associates assigned to those clients. We can decide if we even want to give the option of renewal or send them on their merry way. We have an influx of contracts lately, which I'm grateful for, but we've never had this volume before; then again, I did not have the volume last year years prior to that. *It's giving growth.* Luke 12:48 always pops up in my head at times like this to remind me that when much is given, much is required. After some deliberation, the two that need act right will not be renewed as of today, so they're done effective next month.

Braxton Holdings is next, thus reassuring me that my day is halfway over. After hearing the recommendations for businesses to invest in, I can't pick between the last two contestants, so we are going to go with them both. Everything else is pretty simple so in a bit I'll head downstairs to the talk with Michelle and Samantha. I give Meaghan the rest of the day off because she was a great help, but I can handle the rest on my own. I forgot I needed to give a nod to Piper. She's still a bit intimated, but she's been doing really well with her assignments. Just because I'm the boss doesn't mean I should embrace tyranny.

I don't want my staff to fear me. I want respect. I lead people. I delegate not demean, or at least I try. I called Piper into my office to have a chat and to extend my appreciation. Unexpectedly, she confides in me. I don't know what it is, but people find it easy to tell me all their business. I don't understand it, but I listen intently. Apparently, she lacked positive female role models growing up, and somehow, we began speaking about mothers. As she shares some of her gripes with her mother, I can't help but feel bad yet grateful to my mom for being magical even with the relationship she had with hers. In this moment, I also took note of what kind of mom I don't want to become. Before I know it, somehow it is decided that she'll be tagging along with me to a speaking engagement on Friday.

After leaving the café, I stop at Target and let Target tell me what snacks I want. *Sometimes you just gotta play the game.* I have this incredible urge to eat snacks and watch my shows tonight. I think I deserve it. When I pull up to the crib, Ravé calls me. I haven't talked to her in so long.

"Hey girl hey"

"Hey Kenfolk, what's going on?"

"Girl, I just got back from a Target run. I got snacks and somehow a new throw blanket and clothes for my babies ended up in here. What you got up?"

"Just finished shooting early, so I figured I hit you up since it's been a while. How's Lawyer Bae?"

"Mmmmm"

"Kendall!"

"Huh?"

"You broke up with him, didn't you?"

"Why do you automatically assume that I broke up with him? And I did not know we were in a whole relationship, so there's that"

"Did you? I know you did"

"Yes, but see what had happened was-"

"Was what?"

"This seems like an attack and I don't appreciate it."

"Mmmhmm, so what's the excuse now?"

"There is none. I mean I tried. I just wasn't feelin' him. I wish I was into him. He had no major character flaws or deal breakers. He's Christian in real life, not just a church person, never been married, has no kids, celibate, successful, giving, kind, and comes from a good family. If I did end up with him and have kids, them kids would be set on both sides. I mean his dad is chauvinistic, but I eat chauvinists for breakfast."

"You're so picky."

"Listen, I can't make me love him. You heard that Tank cover. Besides he was looking for his rib and I'm pretty positive his rib is not me. Mmkay!"

"Well, I guess I can understand that. Are you going to get back out there?"

"Nah, not right now. Shucks, I wasn't out there before. Lawyer Bae, as you call him, was just very persistent, plus if the other negroes are what's out there I'ont want it!"

"Ha! What negroes you talkin' about now?"

"These old niggas probably living off of their Pinchin and 401k and getting Social Security before it runs out completely. People don't even have Pinchin anymore, so you know that's old! This old man in Target gone roll up on me trying too hard. I looked at him in the face and said 'Listen, Baby Boomer. You cannot talk to me. It ain't happenin.' And if one more of them old deacons hit on me, I'm gone have to tell Jesus to turn around fa about five minutes."

"I'm crying! Baby Boomer!"

"Girl, yes! Niggas older than my Daddy!"

"You a mess."

"Nah, too through is what I am, but for real, I don't want to be in a relationship right now. If I'm honest I'm scared I just might be good at it."

"What? Wouldn't that be a reason to be in one?"

"Yes and no. I mean 'good' might be reaching a bit. *I mean I know I'm not always a treat but I'm neva a trick.* I don't want to invest too much of myself in something temporary. I've had a glimpse of just how much I would be willing to offer the right person and how being truly invested in someone would change me in some regards and honestly that frightens me. So issa pass for me for now dawg. I'm perfectly okay with being emotionally removed. Now let's talk about you, sheesh. How's my homeboy?"

There are very few things that I'm heavily emotionally invested in, and as dysfunctional as that sounds, I'm okay with that. I like being in control, but it is limiting I must admit. Though love is not an emotion, as it is far above, when in love, emotions get out of whack. They can strongarm anybody and I need a good reason to let them jokers awaken. I know that sole experience just scratched the surface, so I can only imagine how insane it would be trying to navigate unchartered territory. Lowkey, having a good dad can cause daddy issues too. That didn't hit me until recently.

What I've learned about men through my endless hours of movies and shows, observing real life, and in my own experience, is that many men will be with women they know they don't ultimately want because it's convenient and comfortable. They may like them, maybe even love them, but not enough to die for them, not enough like Jesus would love the church. Not all men are whoremongers, but it's some hoe stuff to let a woman waste years of her life fully knowing she's not your wife. Now women have a responsibility too, because just being with someone out of loneliness or insecurity is just as bad. That's the chick I don't want to ever become.

After we are done talking about boys as if we are not grown women with whole lives, I tell her about the speaking engagement I have coming up and of course we talk about her being an auntie soon. She has a gig overseas approaching, but she'll be back in town not long after that to see her people and to talk business with me about Faith & Food.

People wonder why even on the show, I do things a certain way. My niche is the art of scratch. That's my lane. Ravé always inspired me to keep that going and to stay consistent with that trait for the show, but the art of scratch is really my lifestyle. As much as I love and admire my parents, I would not want to model a relationship after their example. They are resilient and wonderful and much more, but there's also a lot that I don't want. Everyone will have obstacles, such is life. Everyone has baggage, but everyone can't help you unpack it. There is some baggage that I am admittedly unequipped and unwilling to help unpack and I'm sure every other honest person will attest to that as well.

Though my dad is a wonderful man overall, he was not always the best example of what a husband should be to his wife. Truthfully my mom, though an amazing woman overall, was not always the best example of what a wife should be to her husband either. Though I value marriage, my perspective of it has been skewed. It's layered *much like everything else about me.* I still believe in it, and I understand that all marriages are different and imperfect, but I want to work on me so that I don't bring unnecessary problems or repeat the history of my parents and their parents. I also don't want to model my kids' childhood after mine. I don't want my kids to feel obligated to take care of their grandparents. Of course, I want them to love them, cherish them, and be around them as much as possible, but in a functional way. I pray that my children get along better than CoCo and I did as kids because memories can haunt you. I know I can't make life perfect for them or her if I just have the one, but I want to set up a life that she doesn't quite have to heal from, not to say that I need healing from my childhood or imply that my parents aren't the best. They know how to raise some kids. They are the epitome of dope parents, but my childhood wasn't what people assume. I'm starting from scratch...

As time flies by, the clock tells me that it is now 1:45am. My speech is now finished, and I need to prepare myself for bed. In what feels like the blink of an eye, daylight has arrived. Another busy day is ahead, but I am grateful. It isn't the norm to wear bright colors to meetings and deal closings, but I am not the norm. *I mean clearly.* With my curly fro on Wakanda Forever mode, I put on a multi-color blazer with a nude tank, my favorite black dress pants and nude patent leather stilettos. I even put on a touch of makeup, and I am ready to devour the day. Today is a Challenger type of day. *I want to go fast like Ricky Bobby.*

After wrapping up my meetings at a decent hour, I remembered I needed to do the café's house seasoning mixes. I vroomed all the way home and changed into fugly clothes to get down to the nitty gritty. Of course, I could have someone else do this for me, but getting back to basics always makes me think and I still enjoy being in the kitchen. Sometimes I just need to be in here to free all that is held captive in the confines of my mind.

...

Walking into this PWI, I am nervous. My palms are like Eminem's when he was throwing up his mom's spaghetti. I try to keep my composure as Piper keeps up with me on this walk down the sterile hallway. *Lord, please guide my tongue.* I become vastly conscious of the large crowd in attendance to listen to my speech as the program director just casually said that approximately 85% of the Black student body is waiting for me. That's a lot of people! I hate to admit it, but sometimes I am apprehensive to accept engagements like this when speaking on matters pertaining to the Black community. It's obviously not because I don't love my culture because I do. *I do it for the culture!* Outside of the normal initial shock when having to do a speech, it's because of my complexion. It's absurd, but unfortunately, there are still people within the culture who will attest my success to my skin tone or attempt to shame me for not being dark enough. This in the grand scheme of things is unimportant, though colorism is real. I may introduce that topic at the next Dope Lady conference. *Note to self: call Akilah.* Today, I'm getting a bit personal as we introduce the daunting subject of money or lack of it.

"Growing up, my parents weren't rich, but CoCo and I never needed for anything, and honestly we didn't want for much. We didn't have name brand everything and had never been taken out of the country as kids excluding Canada, but we never went to bed hungry, we went on vacations, and we went to family reunions. I lived in the same house from birth to my early twenties, so I didn't have to fear if I'd have a home to go to and my parents were in no rush to kick me out of the nest. I was ready to go, but many of my counterparts did not and still don't have that luxury. Staying home even after college or well into your twenties without paying rent is not common in the Black community. There are a myriad of reasons for this, but limited resources, systematic oppression, and more make the list. However, there is one reason that most don't consider -the generational curse of materialism. So often in the Black community especially, we look at objects with little to no value as everything. People don't realize that buying power is more than just buying up the store. It's in ownership, credit, the ability to leave inheritance, legacy. Money is a representation of power; and buying the latest gym shoes every single time they drop when you can't walk in a bank and get a loan no problem IS a problem. When I have children, they will not have the latest everything. I have nice things, but nice things do not have me. I'll get them beautiful items, but I'm setting up trusts. I'm teaching them financial literacy. No child of mine will be another nigga with a broke mentality. Now I'm not struggling check to check, but I'm not wealthy either, so I work hard enough to where when I meet Jesus my kids will be taken care of. If I succeed as a mother, they won't piss it away in a month. It'll be lasting through generations hopefully until the end. That's one of the problems of today, no one thinks about the future. Instant gratification is just that, instant. In financial literacy and as a Believer, I know the importance of sowing and my children will, too.

Whenever I went hungry, it was my fault. It was pride because I could've gone to my parents or my legit friends. I wasn't always cool with staying with my parents in my early twenties, but I had to keep reminding myself of the plan. Though I didn't pay household bills, I took care of myself. When I became a full-time entrepreneur, I was making pennies. I did not have many steady clients and Dope lived off of me. I was doing the best I could. I struggled in silence. It was rare when I asked for anything, but every now and then help was forced upon my stubborn self. In retrospect I was quite the dummy because I didn't have to struggle as much as I did all because of pride and shame.

I constantly learned the hard way, but in time I got it. I kept reviewing the plan and studying financial literacy because I knew my hard work would pay off. My goal was never to be rich and it still isn't. I just wanted to live and support myself, while building for my future children and striving to make a difference in people's lives. Pride and shame robbed me of some peace of mind because I let it, but you don't have to do what I did. I know many of you are thinking, we don't have parents like yours, or you might be embarrassed because you've never studied financial literacy and all sorts of other things, but we all deal with pride and shame to some extent.

There are people in this room struggling to eat who live on and off this college campus. There are some people unsure how to build credit or unaware of how they'll pay off their student loans. Some of you may not be able to go back home when you leave here. I don't know all of your stories. I won't pretend I do, but I was in college once, too. I am prodigiously aware that not everyone has story-book parents or family to support them while they try to figure out life, however, there is help. I'm not naïve enough to believe that everyone will have the same cash flow and credit lines. I won't sell that lie, but I do believe that if we change our communities everybody can live, not struggle to survive.

 I am not a prosperity preacher or a get rich schemer, I just like to see people eat. This is attainable if the community reassembles the village. The foundation needs to be corrected, love must be restored, learned ignorance must be reversed, and financial literacy must be taught.

This will not happen in one conversation, it won't happen in one room, but the domino effect is real. Let's break some stuff up and make some noise. I am honored to have been invited to speak to the Black student body of this university and I am at a loss for words at the privilege of returning to finish out this series on how to brighten our community. This is just Part 1, wait for 2! I thank you all so much for your time."

"Ms. Braxton, you did so well..."

"Call me Kenny. You don't have to be so formal or so nice that you can't be honest. Thank you, but what did you really think?"

"I think you got the cogs turning for some people, including myself. Can I tag along to the next session?"

"Yeah, I like to have a team member come along, so that's perfect. Thanks."

...

As I'm heading to the café to check in with Sam and Michele, I pass this young lady. I've passed her a couple times. I gauge that she has no place to go, but I never see her begging. She doesn't even seem to give eye contact. I keep emergency snacks in my cars for when I forget to eat and have been out all day and for times like this. I open up my arm rest and see a bottle of alkaline water, dried fruit, and granola bars. I pull over and park nearby; when I go sit near her, she's almost startled. I introduce myself and she shyly tells me her name is Natasha.

"Well Natasha, I don't know you, but something has drawn me to you. I'm not sure if you need or want this, but I'd like to give you this."
"I'm not hungry."
"Well just in case you get hungry later or you can pay it forward."
"Why are you talking to me, being nice to me? People usually ignore me. I'm not bothering anybody."
"My mom taught me that sometimes it's kind just to be kind. I have an offer for you. You don't have to take it. I own a restaurant and I'd like you to be my guest. When you come in, tell a team member

that you're friends with Kenny and you'll eat free. No one will know how we met unless you tell them. I have a short list of family and friends who always eat free at my place. Here's my card, my cell is on it if you ever do need anything. If I can do it, I will. If you take up my offer, show them this card if I'm not there. God bless you."

She didn't have any words, but she did accept my card. I hope she uses it. I have an inkling about her. This isn't the norm for me but it feels natural. Mama and George Shunger didn't have a lot, but what they did have they shared. My Daddy is a giver by nature and Mommy is a giver by heart. My family never liked to see anyone hungry. Honestly, some days I think about the state of the world and inwardly weep for humanity. Some days it's unbearably heavy. I cry out to God and wonder why so much suffering. I get frustrated because I think I have to take on the problems of the world and then feel bad for complaining about the few inconveniences I've experienced. I have to take a step back for perspective and get back to tending to my part of the garden, which is why what I can do and what I am compelled to do, I will. I don't want to look like a good Christian, I have my bad days too, but I want to actually try to live the life I preach about and just be a good human because living is hard sometimes. I just want to love people because it's good to do so and it's my charge. Everything I do doesn't require a return or accolades. Momma was right, it is kind to be kind.

"I told y'all before that I'm not a prosperity preaching type of chick. You will not hear me say that everybody in this room will be rich or wealthy. Everyone is not equipped for the same things, and everyone cannot handle the same level of responsibility, including that of monetary nature. I don't know if you all are Believers, but we all foster various gifts and levels of accountability. If you cannot manage $20, how do you expect to handle $2M? Your wealth is not just for you. Some of y'all won't get that right now, and that's okay, but please know that whatever your vice is now, with more money comes more access. Don't let the money mentality get you in trouble. I don't trust folks who will do anything for money and are never content because there will never be anything they won't do to get it. They will do whatever to whomever and I ain't with that, so yeah I've passed on contracts that ain't been *good* though they were lucrative. I believe God got it. He's faithful even when I'm not, so I don't chase every dollar or have a ruthless pursuit of wealth.

Before I start preachin', let me get to it. There are varying levels of wealth and I'd be remiss not to acknowledge a few. Hood rich vs rich. Hood rich people have materials, most of them frivolous and hold no real value. Those materials of the hood rich typically only depreciate, meaning they have no real assets. Detroit playa whip in the driveway, but don't own a home and purposely living above means is the behavior of hood rich. Rich has assets, building financial portfolios, 401k or IRA, investments, rainy day funds, etc. Rich live comfortably, typically own the home they live in and possibly other property, have disposable income, maintain good credit, and build a foundation for future generations, but still need to work.

Now new wealth has surmounted much more disposable income, building for generations to come, may possibly build up to not having an absolute need to work. Wealthy, as in old money, maintains wealth and is able to live off of interest because the insane amount of money in their financial portfolio makes enough interest annually. They come from generations of trust fund babies, and they know to invest. When I use the term invest, I am not just referring to stocks, bonds, and trading. No matter the motives, old money typically has charitable organizations and diversified assets. Again, regardless of motive, they know the responsibility of giving.

Personally, I do not identify with any of those, but we as Black people need to understand the need to plan. Evaluate yourself. Do a full SWOT analysis on your skillset, factor in your education, envision the kind of life you want to live and take into consideration quality of life. Do you see yourself with a family? Yes, you can have a fulfilling career with a family, but is it flexible enough to meet the needs of your family? Are you okay with working 80 hours a week? Do you want to be an employee or employer? If you want to be an entrepreneur, do you see a mom-n-pop shop or conglomerate? If you just want to be an employee, what kind of company are you seeking to be a part of and what kind of growth are you seeking? All of these questions are important when planning for the path of your personal success because there is opportunity cost to everything. You want to be rich, but does your passion lead to that? Some people are rich in heart because they do what they love, they manage money well so their income to debt ratio is phenomenal, but they don't have exuberant amounts of disposable income. However, they have rainy day funds, they live comfortably, and their families are taken care of well. Think about what is important to you. Yes, we need money and there's nothing wrong with hustling to secure the bag, but how are you hustling? And honestly, I hope money is not the most important thing to you because there's no foundation in that.

Before I go, I'm obliged to speak on this. Last time, I spoke about the need to reassemble the village. I meant that and I'll sing that until I see it or leave up out of here, but the village is not the government. A lot of people like to milk the system. Some just don't want to do better. The more we ask of them, the more "freedoms" they take. Our children are not safe the more we allow this cycle of foolishness to go on. If you need a hand up, by all means do what you need to do. We all need help sometimes. I'm not here to shame anyone -myself included. That's not my place nor my desire. The system was first designed as temporary assistance to families while fathers were at war, but it evolved into an oppressive mechanism designed to ravage Black families.

Family is arguably the most powerful unit on the planet, thus destroying the family unit was the way the Black community has been devastated. This is why villages are so important because they intertwine us. The neighbor on your block may not have kids of her own, but she was the neighborhood daycare for families who couldn't afford it. She raised kids, but now she's elderly and withering. Who's she to depend upon? Who's got her? The system or the families she raised? The reason it is so hard to get financial literacy in our community is because we do not support one another. Even the "crabs in the barrel" mentality was institutionalized. They offered so little opportunity, it was drilled in our minds that if somebody gone make it, let it be me, not let it be us, not let us break barriers and kick walls out our way, or let's make our own. I'm not up here to be anti-anything, but if we want to grow that means we must want all of us to grow. It's paramount that we look out for each other. The system won't have us like we'll have us. I got y'all and I mean it. That's my time folks, but please let's connect. God bless you."

As I stride out of the university my mind revisits the concept of ownership, I am overwhelmed with gratitude. I was raised knowing the importance of home, and as a Black woman in America I know the significance of having something with your name on it. My paternal grandparents never bought a house. Years ago, around when George Shunger passed before gentrification was apparent, it was already in the works. My father was swindled out of his house that I knew as my grandparents'. The house needed to be torn down due to all the damage. Daddy wanted to keep up the land and stay compliant with taxes so he could later execute his plan to build it up for something greater for generations to come. It would have been an extraordinary legacy, but the city officials said no to a visionary. Bureaucratic red tape swindled Daddy out of what was his. This was a prime example of the exploitation of locals for the advancement of gentrification. How could he afford to fix everything wrong with the family home, keep up his own home, and take care of all of us at the same time? To this day, it saddens us, but the legacy of that house on the Northend lives through my café.

Finally, I pull up to the complex. As I walk in, I am pleasantly surprised to see Natasha. I decided to say hello before heading to the kitchen. I still don't know much about her, but I know she has a story and for some reason I am inclined to hear it.

Last week's chef's menu regular's pick was a total rush and Chele truly held it down. I have to do something for her, and Sam, too. Taking inventory, I see that I need to re-up the signature spice mixes and sauces. It's been a long day, maybe I'll go take care of that at home.

...

Sometimes you gotta listen to them Blues. I sit and think about George Shunger. He'd turn off the tv and play his music. I put on Bettye Jo. She had the corner house on my grandparents' block. Her granddaughter and I grew up together. She appreciated my raspy voice as a child. I reminisce as I cling on to her unmatched, raspy vocals as a lifeline.

George Shunger loved the Blues and he was friends with one of the greatest before he was a household name and legend. My granddaddy always told me as a child that he could've been a Blues singer and Mama would joke and say he just needed to know how to sing or play. For the life he lived, he had a lot of material. Sometimes I think maybe I should've been a Blues singer in his honor.

While each note snatches my edges off, I mix. I mix away my cares and my shoulders relax. I'm grateful that this hasn't just become hard work for me. It's still my love. It still makes me want to sing my heart out while I pour out love for people to eat, but now I'm beat. For once I may actually shut down my personal cell for a while, too. If it's an emergency, my family can call the landline. *I'm shocked landlines are still a thing.* I think tonight I'll just chill. Tomorrow I have to prepare to teach Bible Study and start reviewing my notes for Sunday's sermon, so I guess I'll have quality me-time. *I seem to have an abundance of that.*

...

I am exhausted. I feel like I'm waiting on some moment, maybe magical, maybe for the other shoe to drop, or just something not in the norm. As the benediction concludes, I can't even think to myself because one of the ladies came to me asking me for prayer. We done prayed at least eight times about the same thing. I know some prayers require persistence, but this sista needs the unadulterated truth right now... *She gotta get a grip.*

"A lot of things happen that ain't right, but you can't sit there and play the victim and still be victorious. You gotta move from the position of a victim. Just about everybody in here has been victimized at some point, but in order to become victorious, you gotta boss up. You gotta dust yoself off and say 'You know what? They did me wrong, but I ain't got time to stay here gettin' bitter. Ima get my butt up and taste sweet victory.' Life ain't fair. That ain't a secret. Our actions affect other people. Everybody, including me, has hurt at least one person this week by our actions whether knowingly or not, so we can't act like we all innocent. The victim has to grow into the victor or else you playin' after so long. The Word does not encourage us to stay in the pit. We are to learn how to get up."

Dang Kenny! She new, too. I hope she doesn't leave the church. Well, I planted a seed 'cause ain't nobody got time to be playin' wit her. She need to woman up.

The morning after preaching be something. People don't really know what it takes to teach and preach the Word of God, the toll that it can take on the body. I might feel real good in the midst then crash when I come down from that spiritual place. I'm going to work from home today and get back at it tomorrow, maybe even Wednesday.

...

My body is shaking from pain, these pain waves have rocked my body, these chills are insane. Rocking myself isn't helping, even in the same direction as the waves. You'd think I could just float to sleep. I'm weak. I'm nauseous like I'm seasick or something. I'm not crying, but the pain is so excruciating my eyes are watering. I was exhausted and battling the normal, teetering slightly out of my normal range, but then this hit. I barely made it out of the restaurant. If this wasn't chronic, I'd go to the hospital. *If I could drive myself, I'd go to the hospital. Live alone, I said. Be independent, I said. Now I'm over here looking stupid.*
Gosh darnit! I forgot I have a family dinner with my mentees in a few days. For the first time in a while I'll have full participation. Normally at least

a couple have schedule conflicts. Well, we might be having someone from the café bring food or we can order in because ya girl can't do it this time. I love cooking for my kids, but it's not looking too likely and my freezer stash won't cut it for all of them.

Seeing all of their faces and hearing their stories from college or the workforce makes my heart smile. Knowing that God used me to sow into them and bring them together makes the hard days worth it. Maybe this is the moment I've been anticipating. Because they know I'm full of it apparently. They didn't buy the smorgasbord angle, but they didn't say a word. They cleaned everything before they left so I didn't have anything to do, and they started a sing-along. I live for a good sing-along, I sing my words daily and get paid to do it sometimes. Hmm speaking of, am I done with filming for a while? I can't remember. My days are so different, they run together. *You prayed for this, remember?* When I locked up, I couldn't manage carrying myself upstairs. It was such a good night, but to put it plainly I feel like trash. I'm just waiting for it to pass.

...

You know what's worse than the waiting room? Waiting in the examination room. Odds are you're half naked, vulnerable in every way. You lay back or sit awkwardly waiting. People are walking by shuffling, so you wonder if one of them is going to charge in the room. You stare up at the fluorescent lights and can only imagine how ridiculous you look. Finally, someone walks into the room, so you feign calmness. You pray for God's will because you don't know what to pray for anymore and you can't go wrong with His will. This isn't the kind of test you want to pass, but you finally want to know the answers, *finally.*

> *"You mean to tell me that a fake disease is slowly ruining my life?! What do you expect me to do? You want me to scream, cry, punch you in the throat? Tell me how I'm supposed to react since a straight face paired with silence isn't doing it fa you! Tell me, let me know how I should react, how I should feel about 'no cure'!"*

As I shake off the memories of that initial diagnosis, I reflect. There are medical marvels such as myself who gradually experience symptoms, or since there's so many of us, maybe I'm not as much of an anomaly as some doctors thought. I've done some research, even talked to some doctors, done much soul-searching so it's already been established that grief or the concept of trauma didn't onset the illness in my body. Many auto-immune diseases don't start with all of the symptoms, it starts with a prevalent one or even something seemingly unharmful, then grows.

One day you sit staring at the specialist and hear "no cure" *but God...* The only thing is that this disease is from Storybrooke. With negative test results and unanswered questions, it's easy for folks to continuously say "trauma makes the body do crazy things." *You know how many times I wanted to slap fire out of somebody for that condescending statement alone.* After so long of hearing that on top of people you love making unhelpful, often unloving comments, you start to wonder. At least, that's how it was for me. I started to despise the whole medical industry, the whole process, including waiting. I was over 21 by the time someone understood that. On a visit at my great-grandma's house, something happened. It wasn't the answers I'd been waiting on, but it was something long awaited that I never even knew myself. For some crazy reason, I opened up to cousin B. She said plainly "I know," and quickly embraced me. Those two words changed everything for me in an instant. She just knew. That's what I needed all along. I was already in undergrad on a timeframe longer than planned. I was diagnosed at least three years prior to that moment. I had been sick for at least seven years at that time, and no one "knew." No one understood why I tried to knock myself out in the 10th or 11th grade by knowingly taking too many pills just to get some sleep because I couldn't take the insomnia and malaise anymore. More people than not told me I wanted attention, I was faking, or I was grieving. Some said I didn't want to feel better, I didn't want treatments to work, and a slew of other outlandish accusations. She didn't ask me stupid or patronizing questions. She didn't try to psychoanalyze me. She didn't try to discredit me. She knew.

Sitting here in this exam room waiting, I wish someone *knew* right now.

"What's it like?" The concern in Brittany's eyes almost looks new. Like it's deepened.

"It's like going to the hospital scared, thinking you're on your last leg or near death then being discharged because it doesn't show up on labs. It's explaining to people why you've been on bed rest for a week or more when just before you looked fine. It's being newly 18 in college, finally getting a taste of what it'll be like to live your own life then having to move back home because sometimes you can hardly walk or function properly so you can't even get out of your dorm just to go get food let alone go to class. It's having old people speculating and children wondering why you have a cane in your car. It's friends you introduced hanging out with each other while you stay home because your body shuts down so much that they barely even think to include you anymore. It's people with your name in their mouth with little to no care and definitely with no compassion. It's laying up after surgery with no visitors, but people calling your phone to ask for favors. It's being excited about something then disappointed in an instant because your body continues to let you and everyone else down. It's lonely because you don't want to be a burden or have people look at you with sad eyes. It's secluding yourself. It's working tirelessly to build something that lasts and to live out this purpose on your life because you don't know when you can't. It's speaking at conferences and appearing to look like you're living the life when you barely live at all. It's having ugly thoughts and unbelievable fears that you want no one else to know." Tears start to form as these words escape the depths of my soul. All the words I usually cannot bring myself to say.

When chronically ill, it's easy for illness to consume your conversations, ergo your life. I typically only speak openly about my health at home or with those close to me. Even then, it has its limits. There have been few exceptions, weak moments even, but for the most part that's it. It still has a way of being present, so oftentimes I try to avoid talking about it even more. I'm trying to be more cognizant of my speech so as to not give sickness more power. I'm trying not to allow it to consume me, and I want to be held accountable for that. On the flip side, I understand that never speaking on it doesn't make it go away and will not make me less frustrated. I'm learning that sometimes it's necessary for me to speak on it for the sake of my mental space, relationships and sometimes it's not even about me. Sometimes I have to be uncomfortable and share it as part of my testimony.

Brittany is one of the few people who doesn't listen to me and does what she will. If I'm struggling and even say I want ice cream, but don't need it, she'll show up at my house with Superman or Pecan Praline. When she was good and pregnant with my goddaughter, she took me to the hospital when my parents were coming back from Chicago because I didn't have anyone else, so I didn't have to call an ambulance. Even today, she's here checking on me while she's growing my godson. Brit has seen me through some days, but I don't think she's ever asked me that. I'm sure along the line a friend has asked, and I've given brief responses or evaded the question because I am who I am. Something was just different this time.

Sometimes it's nice for someone to show up without me having to ask. I know I'm many things including stubborn, but my people know me by now. Outside of my parents, I don't really have anyone in my health support system. Much of that may very well be by my own doing, *okay fine much of that absolutely is,* but my friends know I'm not going to say I need something often. They know my cry for help. I wish I was more okay with being seen as vulnerable. I only truly trust a few and even that has its limits. *Clearly, I mean here is Brittany threatening me if I don't call and ask for help.* As pushy as some are, sometimes they don't push enough, or push correctly rather. At times, I don't know if I don't allow people to show up for me or if they are simply incapable of giving me the help I need. Often, the first reigns true. As I go through my mental rolodex, I don't have many friends at all. I am friend to more than who are friends to me, and that's okay, but sometimes it isn't. I'm recognizing more and more who is in my village and when I need to put my mask on first.

I'm no martyr. I don't like pity and unwanted attention, but sometimes I just want someone to say, "I see you, I understand," not tell me about how their auntie's sister cousin friend had the same thing but it turned into something else. I don't want advice on what I should do because Lord knows everyone knows something when they really know nothing. I don't want the rude, condescending comments, the quizzical looks, the pitiful stares, and so on and so forth. I want someone to say I got you. I know it's not life-threatening like cancer or something, but I'm sick every single day. They can't cut anything out to fix my body and make me feel better. I'm not 30 yet and I have been sick most of my life now. I don't remember what it's like to not fight sickness, even before they started giving it a name. Flare ups can be so bad that I literally want to die. I never try to let my mind go there, but it's hard not to when struggling to function. I fight every single day and some days it feels like I'm losing terribly, like I'm no competition, like I ain't getting licks in at all. I know it could be worse and people are suffering all over the world, and that selfish line of thinking is terrible. I know God has the last say and God is good. I'm aware that nothing can take my joy without my permission and that God gives a peace that surpasses all understanding, but I am human. Some days being human gets the best of me. Then, I remember my why. I have a vision to see forth and I'm not just the sick girl in high school from ten years ago anymore. Now I'm the one crushing odds. Most with my diagnosis don't work in their desired fields, but I created my own. I've built my businesses from the ground up and I'm still growing. I'm a self-taught chef with a whole show. I sow into people daily. I get paid to motivationally speak and inspire others. I preach and teach the Gospel of Jesus Christ and encourage people to live out God-given purpose. I'm a dragon, so I'm gone be a friggin dragon. I'm about to have a whole kid, so these little moments where I forget who I am have to stop. *I guess homegirl isn't the only one who's gotta get a grip.* That time is coming.

As I wake up this morning, remembering that I'm a doggon dragon, I reflect on this warning this minister gave me. I was one of the speakers for this women's day event at a Baptist church. As I was leaving out with a danish in my hand on a mission to get to the preachers' meeting, I was stopped. The minister said she didn't know me, but wanted to leave me with something. Essentially, she told me that I needed to remember Whose I am and that I am not my own. I didn't give myself these gifts. I don't quite remember what she said verbatim. Her statement wasn't accusatory, but I knew it was divine because it was confirmation. When you're in line with the Spirit, prophesy isn't typically new information, rather it's confirmation. Another way to try their spirit is to simply see if their words line up with the Word of God and His foreseeable plan for your life.

It's easy to start thinking that you are the one changing people, when really it's God doing the changing. Sometimes when we reach new levels and get a taste of what's exotic and expensive, we act a little different. Confidence can then turn to arrogance. Arrogance can easily make us our own god. We begin to demand stuff instead of being used by God and allowing Him to give the increase in whatever capacity He sees fit. Sometimes we forget to take the way out, the escape. Even if we don't show that idolatry, we indulge in the thoughts. Not all thoughts are our own. The enemy does play mind games, but what we entertain -that's when they become ours.

Lord as you develop the gifts you've bestowed upon me, develop my character and remain my foundation. Please remove what's in me that's unpleasing to You. Please give me a repentant heart. As you transition me into a mother, I pray that you guide me to train her up and instill values that reflect You. Build me up and make me fearless to protect her with my life. Regulate my mind and allow me to be mindful to revere You giving You all the honor You are due. In Jesus' name. Amen.

...

May 31, 2022

At this point, I've met with her numerous times. I've stifled my excitement. I took baby steps. We've had visits. She's been to my home. I took her to Kelsey's birthday party this past weekend. We've gone out for ice cream. We've talked about a lot. She'll be ten in June. She loves to read. She's wildly intelligent. Her natural hair is full of tight curls. She's tall and graceful. She'll be so statuesque. Her name is Renee Tiana. Upon legally adopting, her last name will be Braxton. Renee Tiana Braxton. That has a nice ring to it.

Now, I just have to ask if that would be okay with her.

"Renee, I think you are an exceptional young lady. I've had a lot of fun getting to know you these last couple months."

"Are you leaving?" She asks, looking up at me with curious eyes.

"No, I'm not leaving, but I do want to know how you'd feel about living with me, making my home yours, too? How would you feel if I adopted you?"

She begins crying. I don't quite know what to do, but I can't stop talking. "You wouldn't have to call me Mom and you don't have to come with me, if you don't want to. But if you want, I'd love to have you." *My eyes are getting ready to do that water thing, too...*

As she wipes her face trying to steady her voice, she says simply "Well if you need the company...". That was her way of saying yes and I can't breathe. I am so happy! *And I mean that response, gosh she's my kid already!* Tears start forming and rolling down my face, and her little hand grabs mine. It's as if this moment makes all things right with the world.

...

Now the preparation begins. We go to court in a few weeks to finalize the adoption papers and make her name change official. In the meantime, a party is being planned for when she comes home. I don't want to bombard her, but it's kind of like a meet-n-greet. I want her to know that she has more than just me. She has an entire village now and everything is going to be okay.

I decide to work from home the remainder of the day and have an impromptu visit from Brittany and my god babies. I haven't seen those little faces in so long. While LiLi is minding her business and Dre is napping, Brit and I catch up and I let her know it is confirmed that Renee is coming home. She's helping with the party. Though I didn't like the intervention with Mommy and Auntie Cookie too much about the single mom issue, with it being real now it's hitting close to home. I know I can still provide Renee with a good life, even if it will be a little more challenging going at it alone. I believe in a nuclear unit, I'm a product of one; and though I'd do a lot of things differently, being from a nuclear family served as a very positive foundation. I'm not having doubts, but the harsher end of this new reality is becoming more apparent. In this instance, it is a choice I want to make, not like before... Before I get completely lost in my own thoughts, I hear all about the adventures of Nurse Brit. I'm so proud of her and we schedule wine

When she leaves, I find myself a little unproductive because I can't help but notice the parallels of this new chapter with the leap I had to take for Ivy. I became an instant mom of a teen who had seen many unspeakable things. The months she lived with us were in one of the worst years of my life. My prayer is that this transition is not like that one. But things are clearly different now. The biggest thing is I'm in my own house, I'm much more than seven years her senior and I am not responding to an emergency. Though my parents will be involved as grandparents, it'll be a lot different. I have more resources and flexibility. When Ivy moved in, my grind was securing clients, I had a side gig that often cost more than it paid, and all around a lot going on with limited resources. Ivy had to take the bus after she graduated sometimes, but my father was extremely adamant about that not happening and quite often fussed about how I never took the bus. For one, my father has had multiple cars for most of my life, my parents were able to work out their schedules collectively or they tapped in the village. Secondly, I absolutely did ride the bus when I lived on campus, but it was out of sight out of mind and admittedly in another city. For obvious reasons, I didn't have a network of moms for carpooling. She had to do what she had to do. I wasn't being a horrible person pushing her off, I was doing the best I could. Truthfully speaking, I'll always go to Nita and Walt for sound council because I'm forever five, but at the end of the day I'm grown and it's my house, and she'll be my kid. Back then I used to say "as long as you live under my daddy's roof, you'll abide by my rules" that was facts, but it had its limits.

It was crazy that not long before I knew the full extent of Ivy's crisis, my Uncle Simon ministered to me and foretold that Ivy needed love and I was the one to give it to her. He told me my gift is love. He said, "I've seen you operate in it, and it goes beyond the pulpit." God always seems to use Uncle Simon to be the one to pour into me. He used to tell me that I had just scratched the surface, but one day I'd see. God gave him insight that I did not fully understand, namely involving Ivy. Her mother had already made me her godmom while we were still close. I showed up for her since I met her, but I did not predict what would quickly come. Even before my assignment became clear, the words Uncle Simon breathed on my life rang and it was serendipitous. It was ordained. A couple years prior to him giving this revelation to me, I wrote a personal mission statement at a job I turned down.

"My mission is to be infectious with love through spirituality, art, business ventures, and everything else I do and am. I want the power of love to advocate for accountability of people. My goal is to see people seek out their purpose and walk in truth. My mission is to be able to reach the unreachable, to teach the unteachable, and love those the world has deemed unlovable. My goal is to be an example of how to live unapologetically and rebuke barriers while learning to navigate in the skin I'm in."

...

As the countdown continues my ambivalence about the reunion gala rises and my excitement for Renee's homecoming grows. After my workday, I'll head to pick up Renee so we can discuss how she wants her room. I want her to feel like she has something of her own. I want her to feel at home here, though I can't truly know what to expect with this major adjustment for us both.

Putting today's meetings behind me, I giddily head over to get baby girl. When she hops in the Ram, it's hopeful. She tells me about her day and what they're learning, some type of new math. It sounds stupid, so I'll be teaching her real math at home. *What the heck ever happened to "Please excuse my dear Aunt Sally?!"* Before I get too lost in pointing out the errors of the school system, I enjoy hearing about her day and I pray that she continues being open with me. I want her to always come to me and know that I will serve as her safe place. After buying nearly everything in the store, I drive home letting my mind free. Ten years may not be all that long, but this little girl will be ten whole years this month. She was born the same month I graduated from high school. If I told 17-year-old me what's going on, she probably wouldn't believe it. I've always been a planner, but I wonder what I thought I'd be doing now back then. I genuinely don't remember too many solid ideas. I had it in my mind that I would graduate, have a career, make my parents proud, and I wanted to get married and have all my children before 30, but then as I entered my twenties, the concept of actually putting myself out there became a real factor in meeting those goals. 30 didn't seem so far away, especially since most of my twenties felt like a blur-not even from living wild. Life altering decisions and goals don't always fit into the notion of age. I knew I'd be a boss, but probably didn't imagine I'd be doing all that I am presently. I always knew I wanted to build a house, but certainly didn't expect how unbelievably fast it transpired. I keep learning that plans are funny like that.

As I pull up to the house and begin unloading the truck, something pulls at me. I continue flashbacking to the experience with Ivy. I was overwhelmed by instant motherhood, especially to a child who was not much younger than I in physical years, but in maturity levels and mental space we were quite apart. I remember writing her a recommendation letter to get into DSA, my second high school. She made it to all the top choirs. I went to performances and was her confidant. I never would've thought I'd be standing in as her parent and pinning her at the ceremony during her senior year jazz café. Before I was her GG, as she called me, a glimpse of a Mother's love was shown to me, but when she came to live with my family and me, I had no clue. Her trauma unraveled more and more. I had to make the impossible decision to call CPS out of good consciousness.

Anxiety attacks. Shaking and scared needing to sleep in my room. Reversing the severe medical neglect to which she was subjected. Monitoring diet. Court case. Massive invasion of privacy. Teenage mentality paired with unspeakable trauma. Nearly every single day was emotionally draining. Being sick on bedrest and taken care of by my mom was a reprieve. *I'm not emotionally equipped. Typically, if I can't fix it, cook it, sing it, punch it, then issa toss-up.* I was out of my depths. ER visits. Canceled plans because of a fever that wasn't mine! Childlike behavior due to childhood trauma. She clung to me as her lifeline. I was her security blanket. I advocated for her and taught her self-advocacy. I made her a part of the family. Whether I wanted it or not, no matter how unorthodox, she became my first kid and I became her instant mom. I had a distorted view of her mother who was once my sisterfriend. Outraged at every single trash person who knew, but did absolutely nothing! A host of relatives, family friends, church members stood by and did nothing, but had everything to say. The condescension toward my youth and my family as a whole by those hypocritical, perpetrating, generational-curse-enabling, self-absorbed, indecent niggas made me want to really share some ungodly words and throw these hands! *Why must I be the one to fix it when I wasn't in it to begin with?! I questioned God about this because I was over it.* I was furious and frustrated and likely some other unprocessed emotion.

I had been connected to her since I met her. It must have been why God had me take her on in this fashion. I paid attention to her even before she moved in. I could feel somehow when she needed me and would send a kind thought or check-in. Ivy always said she never knew how I knew what she needed right when she needed it. I didn't know how either, but I just felt it. I felt when she was anxious, sad, scared, and upset. It all weighed on me. I did in nine months what should have been done in years, but the trauma later came with the choice of trouble. It came to a point I didn't know when she needed me or just wanted my attention. My parents, CoCo, and Danielle were there for her, but it was on me. She was possessive of me and even more so when she came to live with us, but the trouble led to her having to leave.

The first time she went into treatment was when I saw marks on her wrists. Somehow God orchestrated it because the day I found out is the day we went. I took her to the hospital and her mother arrived shortly thereafter. Before she arrived, I encouraged Ivy to "tell the nurse in triage everything you told me..." When it was time, she called for me to sit in with her, not her mother, so her mother left. In my final semester of undergrad with assignments due within hours, I spoke to a social worker alone trying my best to do what was right while still not wanting to cause trouble for her mother. Days later, her mother asked if I'd take her in, but before I gave her an answer, she changed her mind. More hurt was inflicted that I didn't know of and more damage was done by the time she ran away. I didn't even know she ran away until her mother called me on some bull, but the funny thing is I knew something was wrong, which is why I checked on her while I recovered from surgery. She didn't tell me any details until after that call from her mother. In a few days' time, she was in my truck.

She told me on numerous occasions that if it weren't for me taking her to the hospital that first time and advocating on her behalf to her mother, she would not have made it. While on bedrest, exactly a week before my birthday, I had to take her to get treatment again. My mother drove as I was still pretty ill. That was one of the worst experiences of my life. Seeing her face. Looking into her eyes. I fought for her life. Consoling her. *The letters.* Nightmare doesn't do it justice. The inadequate psych care. The sheer incompetence. The calls. The tears. The shaking. I screamed in a way I never had weeping like a mother with a dying child in the hospital. At the time, she was my dying child in the hospital.

On the milestone that was my 25th birthday, I was alone weeping over a child that was never truly mine. Even if I had plans, I couldn't have celebrated with my baby in so much agony *and she made sure of that.* I still remember the phone call that night. Instead of partying with friends or being wined and dined by a handsome young sir, I was trying to keep myself from falling apart because I had to fight for her. The storm was not letting up. Everything was just too much, but then quite frankly sh*t hit the f***in' fan. *Yeah, that bad. Drove a preacher wild. Lord forgive me.* I was overwhelmed before and draining myself so terribly that it was killing me. I could feel stress being introduced to my already compromised body. Overwhelming concern took a backseat to betrayal. It's some heavy stuff for someone to tell you that you're the only reason she didn't kill herself and then have to put that person out of your house. The falsehood and manipulation got out of hand. I was now unhinged. I was slapped in the face and everything my family and I did for her was pissed on. Cussin. Fussin. Ready to box is putting it nicely. Being ganged up on by my uncle and aunt while my dad was a part of a highly unnecessary and inappropriate conversation. None of them had all the facts and none of them knew her like I did. I thoroughly believe that no one other than God loved that girl more than I did at that time. Not one person in that room would have done what I had done in my twenties, but they had all the words to say when I could and would no longer do it. I think my dad being a part of the conversation was the kicker. That hurt the worst, and then still being in a dependent position only added insult to injury. The hits continued with foster care dealings. A legal case was being built against me. Nearly cussing out the psychiatrist who had me plenty messed up. Phone calls with people I never alerted were curious as to why. Even in the midst of the foolishness and being harassed for months and months, I still protected her when folks chimed in on what they could not fathom. I had to put out my first kid. Yes, I was tired, but I would have kept on pushing and fighting for her if certain events didn't take place. That was a kind of grief I wish on no one. She needed more help than I could provide at that moment.

It took all of me not to smack fire out of her when she looked me in my face and said she saw how it was breaking me down just like it broke her mother down, when if her mother truly broke herself down for her and her sisters, she would've never been under my guardianship in the first place. That was the nail in the coffin, so I thought. As time passed, more nails were drilled.

There was a time when we were all playing around at the house, my Kelsey was there so we were all rough housing, just playing and having fun. Ivy made a statement that she could take me for real. *I should've seen something then, but I let it slide.* When everything hit the fan, I would've gladly let her find out that I'm truly the wrong muthaf***a to f*** with. Unfortunately, I'm no stranger to anger issues and that season certainly did a number on them. *Not always the best example of a preacher, but what I am is real. I'm self-aware enough to know I got issues and love Jesus enough to surrender to Him and work on those issues to try to live up to the standard of His Righteousness.*

It got to a point when I couldn't even be angry anymore, I was just straight up done. There was no way that things could ever go back to how they were. She was legally an adult and I no longer had to be the mother she needed. Her family failed her. There were generational curses. Somewhere along the line, her mother was failed, too. It wasn't Ivy's fault that she needed to live with us, but it was her fault that she was no longer welcome. It nearly killed me to kick her out, but trust was lost and truthfully it was best that she left. I prayed that she got the help she needed as I tried to let go of the anger and disappointment. I felt for her, as everyone else did, but I had to feel for me. I had to save myself, really my mom made sure of it. I put her out, but Nita said she could never return. Contrary to what some may believe I do not believe nor make everything about me, but real talk it was messed up how most people in my life had no regard for my well-being. It was only my mom and a very small handful of loved ones who made it a point to check on me, not ask stupid questions or try to guilt trip me about what they could never understand.

Initially, I just needed time and planned to have some semblance of a relationship, but one morning when I could hear over the noise, I just decided a clean break would give me peace. I was more than content knowing that she was getting better from afar. Folks asked how she was after and for details of where and with whom she was, but I couldn't ask even if I wanted to because it was no longer possible for me to be that invested.

She had to do her, and other people were going to have to pick up where I left off on her journey because ours together was done.

Months later, after the dust settled, I knew I had to say something to her. It felt like she needed to hear from me. I'd barely said anything at all to her. I sent her a text. I didn't need nor really want a response. I would've sent an old school letter, but I had no current address and clearly wasn't asking for it.

> "Dearest Ivy, my silence doesn't mean I'm angry with you or haven't forgiven you. I'm just satisfied with knowing you're okay from afar. I'm still thinking of and praying for you. Please make sure you're mindful of your total health and advocate for yourself. You are a shining star and I look forward to the day I see your name on something incredible. I pray more so that you are so deeply rooted in Christ that you cannot be swayed by any of the temptations and baggage often associated with your gifts and college. I pray that He is evident in your daily walk and decisions. Even with how things ended, if I went back in time, I would still make the decision to advocate for you over again because you needed it at the time. I love you; I always will."

Regardless of her age and what happened, I lost my first child. I would never compare that experience to a mother who had a miscarriage, still birth, or loss of a child at any age. I wouldn't disrespect anyone by even allowing that to sound as if I experienced that magnitude of loss, pain, or trauma, but a loss I did endure.

Months later after sending her that text, for ministry's sake, I entertained a conversation she apparently needed. To be truthful, it pissed me off all over again. The enemy tried to reopen old wounds, but initially I thought if it helped her then glory to God. After it sunk in for me, it only highlighted more things that did not add up while she was still in my care. It exuded ungratefulness and blame seeking. That's what got me. After reflecting on this conversation, I had more to say to set the record straight, but it would have been a thorough waste of my time. So, instead of having an ought with her, I simply had to have a come to Jesus moment and ask His help to truly let it go. I accepted that if I had to be the bad guy, then so be it.

There was a little girl involved and the system failed her. That's why I had to make the ultimate decision to call CPS and not just let Ivy ride out until 18. It also provided more resources to Ivy. Her baby sister's outcome was not my fault, and it was out of my hands. I was going to take her in before all hell broke loose, but the system no longer allowed it after the same system asked me to consider it. I live with that every day. I, however, refuse to carry the weight of it. I don't have a problem acknowledging when I'm aware that I'm wrong and being accountable, but what I won't do is be accountable where I'm not at fault. There's enough on my ledger, so I don't have time to add on anybody else's bad blood.

What's crazy is it's a known fact that when calling CPS, the end result very well won't be ideal. When you know the risk of calling CPS and still deem it better than the parent or guardian the child is with already, that's a freaking terrible situation, and I don't wish that responsibility on anyone. Ivy was mad I did not tell her beforehand, give her a heads' up so to speak, but she didn't share this until well after. That would have made a tough decision even more impossible because she would've begged me not to, ran away again and possibly even worse. She was a suicidal runaway when I got her, so what would I have looked like sharing that weight with her? She already couldn't sleep at night. She feels like I betrayed her trust, but what I did may have saved her sister's life. That little girl was in so much danger at that time, there was no real choice, so I made the adult decision without consulting the child in the situation. Though Ivy was dang near an adult in the eyes of the law, she was my child in that moment. She was upset because she was bombarded by family feeling the need to explain herself, but if they were worth any explanation at all, they'd be asking the adults who inflicted or allowed the abuse, not a traumatized teen. They all failed her, every single one of them, and she had the audacity to be upset with me, but I've learned people can feel however they feel. I won't pretend like I was perfect. She wanted me to be accountable for the wrong thing. I will not hold the weight of the cruelty and abuse inflicted on her and her sister, when I would've died for her. When she asked if it was because she needed help or what she had done as to why I put her out, I can't even explain how I felt. There is no singular word in the entire English language to describe it. She never knew me at all if she had to ask me that question.

...

I'm always learning to never regret loving, no matter what capacity, be it storge *family,* philia *friendship,* eros *romantic,* or agape *how God loves.* Even seemingly unrequited love can heal. And even when terrible results come after sharing love as it did, love can cause growth and eventually healing. We can always make room for more.

As a believer, I often sang my life is not my own with great conviction, but when I actually had to live it in a way that I did not ever expect, it was hard to sing it with that same gusto. There are many things that I can admit I was not the best at, but truthfully I was put in the position that I didn't want nor know how to manage. I tried very hard not to become resentful of the decision that I made. Even as time progressed and everything hit the ceiling, it was the right decision. Frankly, I didn't think I had a choice.

I suppose in a way I adopted already, but the lines were blurred for many reasons. I sacrificed for her and was protective of her. No matter her age, she was mine, then she wasn't. I know it'll be different this time around, but I'm praying my journey with Renee doesn't end. I'm also different now, more prepared-I hope.

As days go by, the parallels of standing in for Ivy recede, and I am able to focus on the here and now. With all the "Mommy prep" I call myself doing, I almost forgot about this ten-year reunion, or maybe I wanted to forget. If it wasn't for Mia Gina, I would've let it bypass. The gala is definitely Saturday. Hmm, what shall I wear? Something that makes me look Michelle Obama-esq. At my high school graduation, somebody else's mama told me I looked like the next Michelle Obama. I hope I never forget that moment. *I ain't e'en know that lady, so you know it was real.* I need that same energy. Her husband asked me where Barack was. *At the time, it was way too soon for a Barack, but now...you know what that ain't e'en the point.*

I think it's time for shopping, maybe having an outfit will make me want to go. I still have a hard time spending on myself, even though before money or lack thereof was definitely the main factor, but it's not like I don't work. I might as well treat myself, especially in my last days before officially having a whole kid. *Note to self, learn some self-care and commit to it.*

As I walk through the mall, I people watch. I take in the novelty of being here, not in a rush to get back in the field or exhausted from a full day, but just leisurely executing my mission to look poppin' at this gala. I somehow managed to not have any meetings today and I'm trusting my team to handle everything. My business direct line hasn't even gone off since a couple of morning calls. This right here is novelty. I'm thinking some kind of snack is in order before I leave. *I do love a good snack, oh that reminds me I'm itching to do a new chef's menu.*

As I shoot a text to Sam and Chel, I walk by this store and a dress pops out at me. It screams my name so loudly that I'm sure the entire mall heard it calling for me. It's this gorgeous gown that's over the top, but not too showy that people can say I'm doin' too much *unless they're haters*. It's just extra enough. The color is a beautiful magenta, the silk is exquisite, and the designer is Black. It pairs with these silver shoes with minimal adornments that go so perfectly with the bodice of the gown. *Inner me is gasping.* I must say, I am an efficient shopper, except for the times I go to Target with nothing but vibes. Not so long ago, I would've shuttered at spending so much money at one time. I love a sale and don't spend extravagantly often, but I'm grateful for the growth. I didn't have to shuffle a few cents around to scrounge up a dollar. I was able to just buy it for myself and that is an accomplishment all by itself. After leaving the mall, I head over to the café. The offices are fine, but I miss this vibe. I chat with some regulars and head to the kitchen like usual. I decide to close with Sam and Chels so we can go over the new calendar and they can debrief me on anything noteworthy. After we chop it up for a while, we disperse and I'm cruising home.

...

I wake up with a calmness and for it I am grateful. The week has blown by. With the gala being tonight, I decide to have a day of leisure. I'm trying to hold myself accountable to not working. I ease in my morning and go hard in my therapy session with Mr. Everlast. I even decide to make breakfast with my tea. I rarely ever make breakfast unless I have guests. Well, soon breakfast will be more of a necessity, as a smedium human will need to eat every morning. I sure do hope we have similar tastes in cereal. After making some shrimp and grits, I decided to do a little cooking, mainly for fun, but also to stock my freezer. I have a few hours to kill before getting dressed, and I have the urge to just enjoy my kitchen. I try to think of comfort food that will make Renee feel at home and loved.

Food is amazing the way it can shape memories and induce emotion. It's one of the main ways I share love, so I really hope my cooking becomes her favorite *or she gotta go hehe*. I make my Tomato Basil Chicken and Wild Rice soup. Even my dad loves that soup, so if he loves it, I have high hopes for baby girl. I also make use of the extra chicken and rich stock for some super delicious Enchiladas. I try to make them as authentic as possible, but it's always a touch of soul when I make it. If we take them out soon, I'll summer those up with a mango sorbet for dessert. It's a little healthier than ice cream, but still sweet and yummy. *Gosh, I'm thinkin' like a mom already.*

After cooking and prepping for the freezer, I am calm and collected, but still try to remember why I'm going in the first place. I already paid for my ticket, so there's that. It will be nice to see a few people I used to kick it with and of course the old squad will be back together. As time winds down, I get dressed and text Mia to confirm her ETA as we're heading there together. Once I get dressed, I look at myself in the mirror and say what rarely ever comes to mind, "Dang chick, you fine!" *Sometimes you just gotta esteem yoself and do a lil dance while no one's watchin'.*

Mia arrives, and with my clutch in hand, I grab the keys to the classic and we ride out. A few laughs in and we're here. *Very happy to see some re-entrification counteracting all the gentrification.* The venue is lowkey dope. We stroll in and pick an exit word for when we need to escape dreaded small talk. As always, we land on 'watermelon margarita.' As the champagne tray passes, we arm ourselves and jump in this sea of people, many of whom I don't really know. I hope some of these folks need my services… *Kenny! Tonight is not about business!* Caught off guard, I hear "I know that's not Kendall!" Then another voice says "Oh, Kendall here? Word."

Nothing good can come of that, and I'm stuck.

"Well, hello fellas. It is I. How are you?"

"Not as good as you girl. Aye…" Such smooth talkers they are. Someone else grabs their attention, however, Grey is still standing before me, so I break the ice.

"You clean up nice. I'm surprised you came to this."

"I could say the same to you."

I haven't spoken to him since I told him it hadn't been enough time. I don't feel any type of way or really anything at all. I'm not even itching to run away from him. I'm past that. I've been able to watch him evolve into the man who stands before me and I'm so happy to see him, but I also don't see a reason to have him in my life anymore and I think he agrees.

"So, you're still going through with it?" he asks.

"Yeah, it'll be official in less than a week. I'm cherishing my last few days before I become a single muva."

"Well you know we could've still made one the old-fashioned way. I'd make that sacrifice for you."

"Boy bye. What I won't be is one of yo baby mamas. On that note, it's time for me to go get some WATERMELON MARGARITAS!" I say the exit word emphatically so Ms. Mia Gina Akens nearby could hear me. *The rest of the room likely thinks I'm a lush now, but oh well it worked.*

I look up and see my lil shawties, the old crew hasn't been all together at the same time in about two to three years, maybe more. After answering, "So, what have you been up to for the last decade?" a zillion times, forcing smiles during small talk, and rescuing friends, them cute little hors d'oeuvres wore off and we headed over to this laid back spot with good eats. It's a gang of us, Mia, our homegirl Lo, Keisha, Shawn, Bre, and more old friends. Everybody here, even folks who didn't graduate with our class. I'm elated to see so many of us doing well.

On our side of the restaurant, food is shared and drinks flowin', but it's not long before one of these hussies tries me. It's too many smirks conspiring against me. Once I hear "prom night" I know it's all downhill from there. *My self-conscious laughs thinking how nothing good can come of this, nothing at all.*

"Ladies! We are sophisticated and accomplished women, why must we bring up ancient history, especially in mixed company?! Who even remembers what happened?! Like what's a prom? It was so long ago, I mean c'mon," I say laughingly.

"Oh, we do and you do, too!" Keisha says, laughing uncontrollably.

Then my homegirls who weren't there that fateful night yell out "We don't!" *Duplicitous heifas!*

"Traitors! All of you!" I say barely audibly because of the kekes.

"Oh, lemme tell you!" All of these heifas are just cracking up, and just my luck Grey walks right through the door as she says this. They all look at me, and I can't help but laugh so hard a tear starts to form.

"I can't breathe! Haha I can't stand you, any of you. To my defense, nothing happened and y'all know that," I say reaching for my libation. "And what are we anyway, in high school? But if y'all really want the circa 2011-2012 tea, I got the stories boo thangs, let's start wit a few fav honeys. I think Keisha gettin' blasted first..." *I was always considered the "good girl" of the group, so anything they have on me from back then is often hyperbolized. Some events were not completely exaggerated, but ten years later, most of it's comical, at minimal they were lessons learned.*

This night gets hilariously embarrassing for us all, and it was so satisfying. For a moment, we got to be carefree. I haven't laughed this hard in so long. I'm trying to remember to laugh more and live a little more. Sure, business is important, but I learn too often that it can't be my whole life and even though Renee will be my life, she can't really BE my life. I can't solely live for her. That would be an utter disservice to both of us.

...

After getting home from church, I review my calendar and Tuesday, June 14, 2022 is blacked out, the official day Renee Tiana becomes Renee Tiana Braxton. The party for her is Saturday. I normally do something for Juneteenth as well, but we'll play it by ear to see how Renee is feeling after the homecoming celebration. I haven't had to do much of anything and have not been alerted on much to expect either, but I'll have a thank you dinner tomorrow after work.

Brittany really spearheaded this, but Lashe, Alexandria, and Niecey have done a lot too. My parents are coming back to Michigan for the summer tomorrow, so they can be here for the court date and the party. I'm not really sure what to expect, but I hope Renee is able to take it all in and not be too overwhelmed. This is a big change for her. So far, we're doing well, but we won't know for sure until she moves in full-time and the judge makes it official.

I padded this week's schedule with more elasticity to hopefully aid the transition. Lately I really do see just how much I work, and some of my late nights at the complex, namely the café, will look a little different with baby girl around. I know I have to be more flexible for her. Thankfully she's not in school currently, so that should help the adjusting period. As I put down my phone, shut down my laptop, and close my day planner *yeah a nigga still uses a day planner TUH DIS DAY* I head to the kitchen to take inventory of what I have and what I want to create as my thank you. I'm making the summer cocktails I learned from BeBe on my last trip to Portland to pair with dinner. It's looking like grilled shrimp skewers, a tossed garden salad with candied cashews and honey citrus vinaigrette, Halibut Piccata with cilantro, risotto style quinoa and grilled asparagus. I'm also thinking mango coconut tartlets for dessert. I might as well barbeque for Tuesday, too, while I'm at it. *Now I'll be the Black parent to find any reason to throw sum'n on the grill.*

After planning meals and heading to a couple markets to get a few things, I chill and take in the quietness of my home. The safety and stillness of this moment engulf me and I'm radiating gratitude. Though my nerves are really trippin' right now, good excitement and expectation overshadow the tinge of fear. *Love is bigger. It casts out fear.*

Waking up, I get into my morning routine and realize that it will look different very soon. I'll likely peek in on my baby girl in the middle of my routine and make sure she's okay and to ensure she's awake before Mr. Everlast and I have our talks. I'll need to consider someone else in most of my decisions because I'll have a little lady depending on me for nearly everything. I get dressed in a gray and white shift dress with yellow suede pumps. My hair is free in all its kinky, curly glory. Because of the dinner tonight, I'm only working a half day at the complex. I head to meetings with Meaghan, Akilah, and Piper to get debriefed on any new projects and address any concerns. Piper has been doing really well and her probationary period has passed, so now I'll trust her with more responsibility and add her to special teams for bigger projects. Afterwards, I handle pressing matters in my office, contact long-term clients with approaching contract renewals and follow up with the pitches that have been sent out for Black Out. When I finish up, Meaghan and I have a side conversation about the recommendations for this next round of investing for Braxton Holdings, Inc. Before I drop by the café, I do a quick one-on-one with Akilah to get her take on a few ideas I want implemented by Autumn. We also plan her vacation because she's overdue for her paid time-off.

Before heading home, I conference with Chele and Sam. I decided to give them both a much needed raise. I could not have asked for a better sous chef nor manager, and I'm going to need them now more than ever. I'm trying to keep my availability pretty flexible for Renee, but I have a new chef's menu rolling out next week, so we'll be here quite often. I'm happy she's not so young and does have a level of independence. I have a plush office upstairs where she can chill, study, do activities, nap, or whatever. I'm not that personal with all of my employees, but there are a few more like family who I'd trust to keep an eye on her. *It takes a village, but everybody ain't in the village. I mean I'm always gone watch my child, but there's a joy and peace that comes with having trusted eyes on her too.* There's a spot in the kitchen where she can chill while I'm chefin' it up, too. We got this.

I force myself out of the café so I don't lose track of time and head home to cook for tonight's thank you and tomorrow's celebration. It's already a couple hours beyond a half day, though still early for me. I put on my apron and get in my element. I throw some chicken, lamb chops, and red snapper on the grill, in that order, for tomorrow. I can whip up sides after court. Now, I'm in the kitchen getting dinner together. My house smells so good. Just as I head outside to clear off the grill and slide on the shrimp, my doorbell rings. My boos are here. Cocktails are ready to go *or as I prefer rets ta go.* I set out the salad and pull the shrimp off the grill and we are ready to eat. Our infamous group chat always comes to life in person and everybody is kid free today. I miss my god babies, but sometimes adult girl talk needs to be fully uninhibited. We all nosey and in each other's business because why not? As I get up to grab my masterpiece, those mango coconut tartlets, the conversation gets good. Niecy is keeping us abreast of the foolishness she sees dealing in the mental health field and Brit lets us know about the life of Nurse B. *I mean honey, this stuff could not be made up.* We schedule our next wine o'clock, and the next time the kids will be around. Renee will have some kids close to her age to play with and everybody loves my little god babies. Mia won't be in town for a couple more days, so I'll do this again for her when she arrives.

Shortly after, I bid the ladies adieu and I go to the kitchen to finish cleaning. I decide to light candles and take a bath shuffling music in the background. I clear my head, pray, and take in the calmness. *I'm finna be somebody's momma.*

More Than Cake

If you look up codependency in the dictionary, you'll see a picture of me with AB, my real mama, *hehe gets me everytime.* She and Daddy becoming snowbirds was good for her. It forced us to cut the umbilical cord. She's still my best girl, but we aren't trapped in the speed force together anymore. She got to reclaim her time after mourning Granny. It forced me to further activate my fierce independence and trust at least somebody in my life to help me when I need it. Most days I still want my mom because I'm forever five, but she's no longer subjected to all of me on the regular. Between CoCo going to college then eventually moving away, my dad's hectic work schedule, my parents' separations, and even after reconciliations, it's been Mommy and me. Sometimes I laugh because all the "manly" stuff I learned how to do: painting, removing carpet, applying polyurethane, knocking out shelves, busting up floors, and lighting the grill; I learned from her. From doing nothing all day to caregiving to emotional support, it's been us...

Mommy and I really didn't have any boundaries, and that's not healthy. I pray that I establish healthy boundaries with my Renee and future children, if I'm blessed to have more. I can't even pretend to imagine that I'll be a perfect parent, only God is the perfect parent, but I want to have a relationship where I can say I need space without lashing out or my child thinking I'm upset with her or I don't like her. I also want my child to be able to communicate with me when she needs space too and provide that to a certain extent, because there are levels to space in a child's development. When my mom needs space, she lashes out like she's suffocating, and in turn I withdraw and become more hardened like my dad. Of course, when the moment passes we're back like never before. Human nature will always have the potential of hurting feelings, even when someone doesn't do anything wrong. I know my children will jump on my nerves and I'll inevitably hurt their feelings, but I want to minimize that as much as possible.

I want Renee and I to have a healthy bond, and of course I want her to want me to be her friend, but when she's grown. I'll always be her mommy first. *Well when she wants me as her mommy. I'm still playing it cool, taking it slow.* She calls me Kenny mostly and every now and then KB and I let it slide.

…

It's the 14th. We are dressed up. She's wearing a periwinkle dress with ruffles and the cutest sandals with a little matching purse. I took her shopping for this momentous occasion. I'm wearing strappy nude sandal pumps paired with a lilac chiffon dress. Being fashionable is important, *just ask Sailor Moon*. The judge's gavel nearly does my undoing. It's official. We're family. Finally, we made it. We head home, *our home*. Everyone is all laughs, smiles, and singing all the way. When we get there, I hand her a bag. She smiles so wide and opens it eagerly. It's a matching denim apron with her name embroidered on it just like the one CoCo gave me. My mini. *Just play it cool, girl.* She puts it on with great excitement and helps me make side dishes in the kitchen. Tonight, it's just my parents and Dani joining us, but CoCo is video chatting us when she's off work. *Her first official family dinner. I got a whole baby now.*

On our first official night, it's only right we watch Gilmore Girls and have a slumber party downstairs. She's so smart and funny. I've seen every episode of this show, so I just watch her reactions. I listen to her commentaries and just take in this moment. It's a wonder I'm not taking pictures right now, but I think I'll always remember this. I sure hope I do.

...

Thursday, June 16, 2022

> "Hey Kenny, sorry to bother you. I know you're working from home this week. Congratulations by the way."

"Thanks, Akilah, what's up? Everything ok?"

"Yes, but I have a favor to ask?"

"What is it?"

"The lady event keynote speaker has an emergency. She's fine, but has to cancel. She apologized profusely, but it's cutting it kinda close to get another speaker to do it within our budget. Will you do it? I know you don't like speaking at our own events, but I promise it's okay."

"(Long sigh), okay. Let me think about it. I'll see if I can come up with something tonight. Send me the theme we landed on, please. Thanks."

It's not even 10am yet, and I've been on calls all day. It seems less hectic working at the complex and rippin' and runnin' the streets than to consult with clients. Oh wait! I forgot, kids do be hungry in the morning, I should probably go check on the kid. I stroll down the hall and open the cracked door announcing myself.

"Hi sweetie, you awake?"

"Yes, I woke up a while ago,"

"I'm sorry, did I wake you?"

"No, I'm just still getting used to being here with you. I like it here -a lot, but I'm used to more noise and other kids."

"You miss your friends, huh?"

"Yeah, I do."

"I'll talk to Ms. Ferrell and see if maybe we can schedule some visits, okay?"

"I'd like that a lot," Her stomach makes noise letting me know it's awake, too.

"You hungry kid?"

"Yes," she says with a giggle.

"Okay, let's go make some breakfast."

We land on a simple, but beautiful Dutch Pancake with fresh whipped cream and berry compote. I don't often make bacon, but seeing that this week we are celebrating, I decided what the heck. I make candied bacon because every now and then I'd like to be the "cool Mom." She's definitely getting vegetables for lunch. After breakfast, I go back upstairs to my office to resume work and set an alarm to remind myself to feed the kid again in a few hours. I have to stay mindful of keeping her fed better than I do myself.

...

You were born a girl and you grow into being a woman, but being a lady is a choice. You have to choose to stay graceful even when you're falling. You have to choose to not be bitter even though circumstances have given you reason. To be a lady is no doubt to be misunderstood, but my dear being a lady is a choice to rise.

Working on my address for the Dope Ladies' event, I'm interrupted.

"Kenny, are you busy?" Renee asks meekly.

"Not too busy for you, what's up?"

"Nothing, I just didn't wanna be by myself."

"If you don't mind me working for a little while longer, you can hang in here and be my assistant, then we can go for a drive or something in a bit. How's that?"

"That's perfect," she says, grinning from ear to ear. *I could watch her smile all day.* Not two seconds later, I get a notice of more work.

"I just got an email that the shoot was moved up. You wanna come to set with me?"

"OMG really?" Her eyes fill with excitement.

"Yes, really. I have to film an episode or two tomorrow so you can come hang out."
"Do I have to be on screen?" She queries with her smile slightly fading. She seems a little nervous.
"No honey, only if you want. You can sit in one of the cool director's chairs so I can see you or stay in the dressing room if you want, I'll ask your Grams to come too."

Renee occupies herself looking through the bookshelves and checking out the pictures and plaques on the walls. While I work, I can peer over at her through my peripheral vision and see her trying not to ask questions. I know being almost ten, it's hard being quiet. *I probably never shut up at that age. Shucks, I barely shut up now.* I try to wrap up and send notes to my teams so she doesn't explode from keeping all her words inside. *It's taking a lot not to laugh right now.*

"Iight, kid. I think I'm done working for now. It's business hours so I may still have calls, but we can go for our drive. We can go to some place for lunch. You can choose, but you're eating something green, and then I need to solidify the menus for tomorrow's shoot. I think we'll go to a few markets and you can help me get a little footage."
"Okay, I'll go get ready!"

She hops up to ready herself for our day and voila we are ready to go. I opted to take the Challenger today 'cause I'm feelin' myself. After we hit the markets, I see I tuckered my baby girl out, so by the time we get home she's knocked out. With her sleep, I go back to the office and tie up loose ends, as I don't work too much on film days. That's work in itself if I'm honest.

Early in the morning, after I engage in my routine and respond to some emails, I do what I seldom do -watch the news. I typically read the news, *if at all truthfully; my why is very layered. Just 'cause we call them conspiracy theories doesn't mean they're all untrue.* Yet again another unarmed, innocent Black child was murdered by a white man who has yet to be arrested. Another reminder of a mother's worst fear. I know I trust God, so there's no need to fear evil, but that doesn't mean it ain't scary.

Sometimes being Black in this country is having a good day or even a regular day dealing with normal life: getting through the workday, being fixated on parenting perfectly, helping someone, thinking about your parents being the new old people, yearning for the presence of your boo, then all that not mattering. It stops mattering because something tragic happened to a child because he or she is Black, and the most tragic thing about it is that it ain't new, whoever "they" are makes it normal. I am now a mother, so the already unyielding concerns of a mother have been multiplied by infinity. It's wanting a good life, but knowing that the "better" you live the bigger a target you are *unless you're an elitist, but most ain't talmbout that.* It can be heartbreaking on any given day. We have to learn how to live anyway. Whether we protest, attempt to assimilate, or address what we can, it affects us in ways we might not even admit. It's exhausting and gut wrenching, but I've learned that you do what you can and try not to carry what you can't. I might not be at every protest and participate in demonstrations every day, but I advocate for the Black youth, operate in Black excellence, promote strong Black families, and align myself with phenomenal Black folks wanting to leave a legacy of untarnished gold. I keep going. I pray over my soul, so I don't become hateful like those who chose to be my enemy and pray bitterness doesn't turn my heart causing detriment to my daughter. I fight every day, and now I have to go be on camera and bring my Black child to set with me.

> "Hey everybody, I know normally cooking makes me happy, but today I need cooking to bring healing. Today before coming to set, I was reminded of the senseless death of a child. The death of

any child is awful, but this child was brutally murdered in cold blood because she's Black. Today, my heart bleeds of anguish for the family of that baby, my blood boils from fiery outrage, and my soul is restless because I am tired. My people are tired…."

I didn't want to kill the vibe of the show, but I had to share the truth if I was going to work through it, and if I have a platform but don't use it, what am I doing? I prayed at the end. I have enough creative control to do that because folks aren't always keen on allowing you to publicly speak on Jesus. Prayer alone won't do the trick, but I know God enough to know that fervent prayer does change things. I've seen prayer change hearts and break down walls.

…

Trying to shake off the effects from recent events and seeing less and less about it in headlines and on timelines, it's about that time for Renee's "homecoming party." I'm trying to get the house together because Mia Gina might be staying here this weekend while she's here for the party. Focusing on Renee's needs and getting her acclimated in her new environment has been keeping me from losing it lately. I hope she enjoys this party, and I'm excited she gets to meet more of her village. We wind down for the night and before I know it, it's morning again.

It's quiet and just the two of us. I opt for fruit for breakfast as today will be a long day and knowing my family there will be plenty of eating. We have a leisurely morning until the doorbell rings. Mia has arrived and I can only pray there are some stories we do not share with Renee. This will be something. After everyone gets settled, we head to the party.

It's breathtaking and the look on Renee's face is priceless. I imagine this has to be a little overwhelming for her, but I think she's happy. She runs up to me and gives me the biggest squeeze and I promise a tear just about escaped. She's amazing and I'm so grateful the way my family has embraced her. Tonight, she's staying with my parents. I don't know who's more excited -her or them. My parents have been trippin' on getting grandbabies for years. This should keep their minds occupied enough to not harp on me being single for a while.

After the party, it's girls' night central at the house. I slick can't believe this. We really the responsible adults in the room. It's been a whirlwind kind of day, and even though I'm exhausted, we're still going to do a little something for Juneteenth. A few people on staff are going to come by and my parents will bring Renee home. Since I didn't have to do anything at all for Renee's party, I'll cook for Juneteenth. It's only right to light that grill up again. Maybe I'll tell her about my grandparents. My sister and I always said we wanted our kids to know from where and whom they come from.

…

June 30, 2022

Today is Renee's birthday, so we're having a family negro spiritual and I let her have a few of her friends over to join us. After cake and ice cream, I let her know she has a surprise coming. She doesn't know we are embarking on a road trip in the morning. This is the first time I really had to connect with other parents. I don't let kids in my home without knowing their parents are in the know, unless in an extreme circumstance. I don't play them games. *And we ain't having another thing at this house for a while. Kenny love the kids, but this a lot. Where Jeepers at?*

By 10, I had been on many road trips-down south to see family, reunions, Disney World, Universal Studios, Canada and trips that I don't even remember. That may not have been extravagant to some people, we weren't going to super luxurious resorts or traveling abroad like many white counterparts, but it was cool with me. I want to take Renee on many trips and eventually

257

I want to take her abroad. Excluding Canada, my first time out of the country was not very long ago. I find myself sharing bits of how I was raised and truly listening to what she needs and expects. I'm solution oriented. I'm a problem solver. It's kind of my job to handle conflicts, but because of my nature, I haven't always been a good listener. I'm trying more and more. To be truthful, many tasks are harder with family because everything always starts with family. CoCo was my first real practice as an adult with active listening. I listened to my parents for the most part. I ain't always want to, naturally. CoCo had to be my practice because there was choice in hearing what she had to say. We had to decide to have a healthy adult relationship with each other. With Renee, I want to make a conscious effort to actively listen to her, what she says, what she doesn't say, how she feels, everything. As her mom, it's my job to operate in conflict resolution, but sometimes kids just need to know they're heard and listened to without fear of punishment all the time. They don't always need you to save their world. She's only 10, but she's still a person and she matters. *Now homegirl ain't gone run my house. That's what baby girl not gone do.* She'll know her place as my child, but I want her to express herself and grow into an independent, well-rounded, well-spoken young lady who learns the importance of self-advocacy.

While riding, she asks me about my life, my childhood, school, all kinds of questions. I normally don't like that many questions, but she still gets a pass. She's still learning what to expect, what I expect of her. Really, we both are. I don't remember very much from my childhood, but there are a few random memories that are still vivid. I'm turning into my father telling my stories to my daughter on road trips. I didn't always spend much time with my dad, especially when my mom moved us out. Even though I was grown, I loved road trips with Daddy, especially when it was just us two because I got to know him more. He told me his version of the night he and my mom met once, days when he was in the service, bits of his childhood, and stories of my Tee and grandparents. We talked about a lot and I mostly managed to avoid questions about my dating life. Now here I am in pure WB fashion sharing stories I hope she grows fond of and learns from.

"From 4th to 6th grade, I was in Academic Games at James E. Vernor Elementary School. I actually loved it. At that tender age, I was very active in extracurricular activities, but this one outside of singing was my favorite. My first time away from home and family for the weekend was for the state tournaments. I was no good at presidents because I never read the book, so always read the book, kid. Linguistics was alright. I was pretty good at equations, a simple game in theory that required great strategy. I was solid, formidable enough I suppose, but I spent most of my energy elsewhere. Woof-N-Proof was my best game. It was the most complex. It taught logic and much more. I can't recall exactly all it taught nor the rules of the game, but I remember it was known as the hardest game. The fact that the hardest game was my best game showed the spirit within me and was more of a foreshadow than I thought. I go after the biggest obstacle. It's not just about finding the biggest thing around to knock it out; it taught me to be the best at everything I do. Not compared to other people, but to myself. It taught me I should've read the presidents book and took a little more time developing equations and linguistics strategies because if I did I would've gone farther. If you have a craft, a passion not just something you do, but truly a trade, something you choose to invest your time in, be the best. Meaning whether 1 or 100, if your name is on it, integrity needs to be the foundation and quality above average work needs to be engraved. I know school is different because everything may not be your passion or your best subject. Maybe you'll join a club just for fun. That's okay, but all I ask is that you do your best and I'll know your best. I'm not requiring straight A's, but if you have that ability I'm expecting that."

"How will you know my best?" she asks meekly.

"Trust me, I'll know." *I'm your mom. I'll know.* I went on to say, "My mom made CoCo and me sign up for so many things and eventually we began finding what we liked and now it was asking her instead of her forcing us. There are a few reasons why she sometimes was overzealous, but she always supported us. I probably won't push you into as many things, but you will have to do some extracurriculars, even if outside of school. They build character."

Soon she tells me more of her passions and what she wants to be when she grows up, and of course it's a thousand different things and I'm here for it. Then we finally arrived. I've lived in Michigan my whole life, and I don't remember going up north much. I think I went as a Girl Scout, but I don't recall, so that's where Renee and I are exploring together. I booked us a really nice cabin and there are lots of activities to get into if we want. We picked fruit and went to a vineyard. Renee is so smart and quick witted. I can't wait to take her everywhere and see how her mind soaks up culture and grows. I'm pretty sure Walt is going to want to drive her out to Arizona soon. *My parents gone steal my baby, I just know it.*

...

We barely got in the house when my parents decided they wanted a visit, so they whisked baby girl off to their house. Now I'm kickin' it solo. Exhausted yet refreshed after my girl Tee's dance class, I set out for my spot. I love getting to go to her classes whenever I can. My schedule isn't always forgiving, but I'm still padding with flexibility for Renee. I hop in the Ram and play some of the songs from today's workout mix to stay hype. I pull up and sit at the counter after I order my food. I look up and to my surprise it's Luke. I'm debating if I should speak, give an acknowledging nod, or pretend he ain't there. He really is a nice guy. The kind of man I wish I was ready to want and truly give it a try with, but I can't help where I am. *Oh dang he saw me.* Before I could decide, he broke the awkward silence between us.

> "Hi beautiful." *I'm still not used to that.*
> "Hi Luke. You look good, how are you?"
> "I'm hanging in there. Busy as always," he says with an expression I can't fully gauge.

"I'm sure you are. I saw some of your mentees in the news. Congratulations. I know you're proud."

"I am, they-" As my phone rings, I have to interrupt.

"I'm sorry. One sec. Hey baby, what's up?" His face shows defeat. I wrap up the call shortly.

"Sorry about that. You were saying?"

"Just yeah I'm proud. They are really working hard and making a difference. I – I presume you met someone?" He just cuts right to the chase.

"Yes, but it's not what you think."

"You don't have to explain." *Duh.*

"I know I don't, but that wasn't a man. That was my daughter." This man's face fell on the flo. *Whew chile.*

"I thought you were-"

"I adopted. I began the process of being vetted for adoption before we met. And I met my baby girl shortly after. It was made official last month."

"That's why you were so closed off." *Sure, let's go with that.*

"To a certain extent, yes."

"Iight KB you all set," the owner says handing me my carryout.

"Thanks love, I'll be back soon," I reply.

"Listen, it was good to see you. Maybe I'll see you around. Take it easy, Luke."

"Can I call you sometime?"

"Yeah sure, we can keep in touch."

I don't really know what else there is to talk about; I don't want to be unfair to him. He's looking for a wife, and now there's a little girl depending on me. She has to adjust to me first. Sure we've had a lot of cake this month, but there's more to digest.

December 1, 2022

It finally seems like we got our own rhythm. The social worker's visits have decreased substantially. I think that's helping us reach a sense of normalcy. We don't have to be on edge wondering how we're being judged while we figure out this new life. She loves my parents and is excited to see CoCo in a couple of weeks. She calls my parents her grandparents and my sister auntie, but I'm still Kenny to her. I don't want to push her, and it's understandable. She doesn't always speak about what she does remember, so I don't know how much she recalls of her birth mother. I do know that when you're not the birth mom, it can still be hard to be accepted. Whether bonus or adoptive, it can be hard clicking, I guess. *I think we're clicking. I hope we are. I'll probably always be a bit of a foreigner to her.* Whether she never accepts me as her mom or not, I pray this is a good home for Renee. *I can't go through losing ano-… I stop myself from the direction in which my thoughts are heading.* This was deliberate. I thought this out and prayed many nights. This was supernatural orchestration. *This has to work… however it does, it is well with my soul. Lord, please lead.*

It's 4:36AM and I can already tell today will be a difficult day. I've been fighting my body and willing it to be functional for months. I've been begging God to get me by and keep me off bed rest. On bad days, I've been able to play it off and just chalk it up to exhaustion from my hectic schedule or too many impromptu workouts. Renee bought it at the time, but today I can feel will be a bigger battle. I don't think I can walk today. I'm having a hard time moving in bed alone. The pain is making my eyes water. It's the kind that makes your body shake. It feels like I could possibly be fighting an infection, too. I'm taking mental notes of every symptom being certain that nothing new is in play. I probably have just been skating for too long and my body is having a reckoning with me. What scared me most about adopting Renee is happening right now. How do I explain a Storybrooke disease to a ten-year-old?

I text Brit to try and catch her before her shift. She's on the approved list at Renee's school. Thank God I have her. I just have to explain to Renee why Auntie Brit is taking her and not me. The tears escaping my eyes were just the body's natural reaction to too many symptoms flaring at once, but now it's crying because I can't get up and I have a little girl depending on me. Every naysayers' words are flashing in my mind about the hardship of single parenting and the reality of my health has multiplied the level of difficulty. *I chose this.*

After repeating my daily affirmation, "Heavenly Father, I believe I am healed. I believe I am being restored through the power of the Holy Ghost in the Mighty Name of Jesus. I believe it is so." I will myself out of bed, take my daily supplements, and throw water on my face to wash away the teary tracks. Heading to Renee's room, I concentrate on every single step with the goal of seeing her face. I force myself not to fall. I defy my own body and try to walk as upright as possible. I finally make it to the door and begin to open it praying my legs don't give away. *Oh Jesus, walk with me. Please.* I take a deep breath.

"Good morning lil mama, it's time to get up for school. Auntie Brit and LiLi are taking you to school today." I am intentional about yielding my voice to sound close to normal.

"Good morning, okay. You have to go to work early?"

"Not exactly, but I will be here when you get back from school."

"You aren't picking me up?"

"No, Big Daddy wants to come get you today, but he's bringing you home. I'll be here waiting for you, okay?" Today, I am grateful that my parents decided to wait until after Christmas to go back to Phoenix. I should probably tell her what's going on before someone else driving her around is more of a frequent occurrence.

"You aren't working today?" I've already sent messages to Meaghan, Sam, and Chele notifying them that I'll be out at least today and tomorrow. She looks so confused. *Lord, help me.*

"No, I'm taking the day off. Now enough with the interrogation Missy, time to get up for school. It's a cereal day, so hurry up young lady so you can eat before Brit gets here. I'll meet you downstairs."

"Yes, ma'am."

She's never seen me use the chair lift on the back stairwell and she's never asked why it's there, so while she gets ready, I try to make it to the chair lift to get downstairs before she notices. I'm not prepared to have that conversation this morning. I have to work on what I'll say to her. I have a hard time getting grownups to understand this, *myself included,* so I don't know how to break this down to a ten-year-old child in a way that's not scary, confusing, or frustrating.

Hours pass by and before I know it Daddy has brought Renee home.

"Hi Kenny!" She sounds happy before she sees how I look. I can see her eyes dim a bit. She must have had a good day at school. I really don't want to talk to her about this when she was just in a good mood.

"Hey baby. Go wash your hands and get your homework together, then I want to hear all about your day." I try to perk up my voice and buy myself a second.

"Hi Daddy, thanks for picking her up." That look on his face is always the same when I'm like this.

"You need anything? You hungry?" He asks eagerly, hoping to help in some way.

"No, I'm not hungry. I just restocked the fridge and freezer, so there's plenty here for Renee."

"You need to go to the doctor?"

"No, Daddy. That won't help today. It feels like I'll have to wait this one out. I just pray it's a short one." *I pray it's not so gruesome for my baby's sake.*

"You sure? You want me to stay?"

"I'm okay, Daddy. I promise. I have to talk to her though; I've held it off as long as I could."

"Okay, me or Mommy will check on you later. I love you."

"I love you, too, Daddy. Be careful."

After Daddy leaves, I call Renee downstairs. I smile and listen to her recap her day. She raves about her favorite teacher and shows me a note. It reads: "Ms. Braxton, it is a pleasure teaching your daughter. *My daughter.* She is respectful, bright, and participative. She is a leader in this class already. Thank you." This note nearly does my undoing. I definitely can't take any credit, but I'm so blessed to have this kid. I hope she doesn't feel cheated like she should've waited on a better family. After she catches some air from telling me all of the fifth-grade business and about her friends, her mood changes a little bit.

"Kenny, why are you still in pajamas?" *Ken, don't lie.*

"I'm tired today." *Well, I am extremely fatigued today, so technically not lying.*

"You don't mean sleepy, do you?"

"No sweetie, not exactly. I think it's about time I tell you something." She comes to sit closer to me on the couch.

"What is it? Are you okay?"

"Yeah, I'm okay," *NO, YOU ARE NOT!* I continue, "But sometimes I get really sick and have a hard time doing things I can normally do. I'm not going anywhere, but sometimes I don't feel well for a while and have to stay in bed because my body shuts down a little and needs breaks."

"Shuts down? What does that mean? There isn't anything a doctor can do to fix it?" She looks concerned, a little scared even. I don't even know if I'm triggering something for her.

"Hey, don't worry. I'm okay. I've battled some issues for a very long time, but God keeps me and heals me. I see doctors sometimes, but they haven't always known what's wrong. A lot of medicines have made me sicker, so I am sure to take really good care of myself. I am a tough cookie, remember?"

"Yeah, you are tough!"

"You're a tough one, too, but I'm not going anywhere hopefully for a very long time. I will always protect you as long as I live. That's my job no matter what. No illness can stop that, okay?"

"Okay."

"Now, homework. How much of it do you have? And do you need help?"

"I finished it already."

"How?"

"We started homework in class so Mrs. Booker could show us an example and then I finished. It wasn't hard. We didn't have a lot today."

She runs upstairs to get it so I can check it. All of it is right. I know everyday won't be this easy, and soon she'll present problems to me that I've never seen before, but I'm grateful for her win today.

Looking at the time, I know I have to peel myself off the couch to get dinner for her. She's independent, but she's still a kid, and I won't place an inordinate amount of responsibility on her just because of my bad days. Fighting the urge to throw this cane against the wall, I grab it to steady myself on my feet. I focus on the task at hand. I think I'll trust her to use the stove if I'm in here with her.

After she finishes eating, she heads upstairs for her nighttime bath. As soon as the coast is clear I use the chair lift and make it back to my bedroom. Her seeing me use the cane was quite enough for the both of us today. When I finally make it to my bed, I hear a knock at my door.

"Yes, baby?"

"Can I hang in here with you until it's my bedtime?"

"Of course, you can." This moment feels like Mommy and me.

She hops on the bed and we watch some of Mommy's and my favorite Nollywood films, well the kid appropriate ones. When bedtime approaches, she leans over to hug me and says "Good night." I muster through my nightly routine and manage to get back in bed. I pray and close my eyes hoping for sweet uninterrupted slumber.

It's now 3 am and I am in my en suite bathroom. I notice the dizziness and weakness is quite pronounced, and before I know it I'm on the floor. I'm fighting to get out of this stupor, but I can't move. I don't know what time it is anymore, but I hear Renee moving. She knocks on the door, but I can't seem to speak. She comes in and I can hear the panic in the way she's rushing. She enters the bathroom and sees me on the floor.

"Kenny, please get up! Please!" I'm trying, but my body isn't moving yet. I'm trying to open my eyes, let alone speak a word. I feel her tapping me and pulling my arm.

"Mom, Mommy please don't leave me. I just got you." Tears are rolling down her face and she lays her head on my chest.

WAKE UP KENNY! GET UP!

I don't know how many minutes it is before I come to, but weakly I manage to speak.

"I'm sorry Renee. I'm okay. I need you to get the phone and call your Grams."

Mommy arrives and gets Renee ready. I'm pretty sure she's traumatized, so I'm not making her go to school today. I use all the energy I have to speak to my baby girl.

"Renee Tiana, I love you. I'll be okay. I'm not going anywhere. Today I need you to go with Grams and Big Daddy while I go see some doctors."

"I want to come with you."

"I know baby, but it's no fun there and your grandparents really need some company today, okay? Can you do that for me?"

"Yes, Mommy." I wipe a tear from her cheek.

"Come here baby girl." I hug her and kiss her on her forehead. "Everything will be okay. I'm so sorry I scared you."

I'm on a gurney and before I'm put in the back of the ambulance, I pass out cold.

...

November 6, 2017

My eyes open. I take inventory of what's going on in my body. I think today will be okay, but I still have to take it easy. This exacerbation was rough. I'm still reeling because my life played in a reel. I must have been really out of it because some of it seemed so real. I've only been able to speak above a whisper for a couple days. I just barely stopped getting winded from only walking to the kitchen. I missed what I hoped to be my last first day of Fall classes in undergrad last week. I've been praying hard, lowkey bargaining with God, to get me through these final two semesters so I can strut across that stage in April. As of the spring, it'll be two whole extra years I've been in school thanks to my health, but I'm determined to finish strong. *I gotta finish or I just might spazz and that's not good for anybody.*

Today, I'm supposed to pick up my last check from my contract position. On paper it was a contract with Black Out, but I was the coordinator, and I was good. The owner didn't want me to go, but when things started turning sour, I knew I had stayed longer than I was meant to... My passion turned into frustration. It was all too overwhelming. I couldn't let her business be my whole heart because I knew I had my own businesses to build. It was weighing heavy on me. The owner and I became close. She worked with me and I with her. My health affected my job there because this position was all consuming, but I handled business from a hospital bed. I still came to work when I couldn't operate half my body. I was dedicated. When she brought on employees to job share with me, I trained them and answered their questions on my off days. I went above and beyond. I had tried to quit before due to my health and trying to garner new clients, but something was different about this time. This was more final. Where I'm from you don't quit a job without having a replacement, but I had to be obedient to Him. When the sting began to recede and she understood more, we agreed that I would still help when needed. I brought her some of my Pineapple Up-side Down Cake and a Pineapple Turnover to show that it's still love; I just had to do what I had to do. Even up to now I've worked over a month since I resigned to help with the transition. Last week was supposed to be my last full week, but her mom forced me to go to the hospital *all because I couldn't breathe and was visibly ill. Tuh, I was totally fine, kinda.* Obviously, I didn't finish out the week as I'm just functional again today.

I finally got out of bed and began getting ready. I put my hair in a messy pinned updo. I hop into some fitted bootcut jeans and land on my comfy, fuzzy sweater. It's white with a couple shades of gray accent patterns. I put on my gray suede boots. I kiss my Mom on the cheek and I'm out. I hop in K Scrilla, a maroon 2003 Jeep Liberty Sport. I take the Lodge and head downtown to pick up my check and try not to get too sentimental with the whole "this isn't goodbye" speech. Each client's name on her roster I know. I can do quality control of her charts with my eyes closed. I was committed to her business, and I acquired many skills, including hiring. I owe so much to Kelley. It is hard letting go, but I got a vision to see through. Soon my days will look different. Leaving Kelley's office, I go straight to campus.

Today when class let out, I opted to head back toward the city. I usually go to Aunt Cookie's house on Mondays so I don't have to drive all the way home to turn right back around the next day. But I have an appointment in the morning and tomorrow is Mia Gina's birthday, so I'm supposed to meet her for drinks tonight. I'm thoroughly exhausted. It is my first full day off bed rest in about a week, but sometimes I like to be 20 something.

When I pull up, some scammer is choppin' it up heavy with her, but I join her trying to steer the conversation away from the weirdo. *This heifa is BEATTTTTTTTT!*

"Well dang nigga, just snatch my edges. Ima be outchea ball headed!"

"HA! Not ball-headed!" Mia responds, laughing.

"Thank you. Thank you!" she says while brushing her hair back.

"We so extra, but what's the occasion? You all did up and I'm all regula degula smegula up in here coming from class."

"I had my photoshoot today."

"Oh yeah, yeah I gotta see the pics!"

After getting a few sneak peaks, we order a round and start getting caught up on each other's lives.

"I did it today. I picked up my last check. I'm officially no longer the coordinator of the program anymore."

"Good! 'Bout time!!! I'm proud of you. I know you were hesitant, but you needed to resign for you." Mia exclaims.

As the night goes on *and the scammer continues talking about whatever he talmbout*, we just unwind for a bit. For some reason I slightly phase out the conversation. I look over to the right, and I'm stuck. *Lord, was he here the whole time?* There is a man within arm's reach sitting there and I am sure he is unlike any other. *Lord, fa real, was this man here this whole time?* I don't even remember what I was talking about two seconds ago. *Okay Kenny, get it together. There's probably nothing special about this man. Am I staring? I don't even stare. This is new. Jesus, what's happening? Does this man wanna have my babies? I need clients, not a boyfriend! Kenny, he has not said a word to you.*

"Oh, so I heard it's a birthday, is it your birthday?" This man just spoke to me. *This beautiful, intriguing man just looked me in my face and spoke to me. Me? I don't know if I have words. I'm just over a semester away from a whole business degree. I own two businesses. I just voluntarily left a position where I spoke with clients, insurance agencies, and staff all day. I'm a preacher, and I talk too much in general, but now I have no words because this man just spoke to me. What the hell!*

"No, it's my best friend's tomorrow, mine is in a couple weeks."

He offers to buy Mia a birthday drink and then extends the offer to me. He doesn't really say anything else and I glance over to see the football game has his attention. I don't know what it is. I'm typically not like this. Of course, I can appreciate an attractive man like the next woman, but this is different. It's like I'm in an outer-body experience or something. *Well maybe not outer body. I can't even articulate the proper terms to myself.* Mia Gina very conspicuously hints for me to give that man my number, but why? My facial expressions explain that he's barely said anything to me *and seriously was this nigga here the entire time?! I need answers.* We have silent conversations with our gestures and it's as if she's reading my mind because she tells me that he's been there for quite a while. Before I know it, he speaks to me briefly. He's an engineer. I tell him that I'm finishing school, but I'm a full-time entrepreneur. I know it has to be something about him because when he stops speaking, I wonder why, then remember the game. I do find out that he isn't a fan of our home team. I'm always coming Detroit Pride, but if I'm honest I can't blame him. *They know they be stressin' us out.* After that fleeting exchange, the drinks arrive, he pays then he and his friend leave. I don't know his name nor does he know mine.

"You need to go give him your number! He was here for a long time and never said anything to anyone until you," Mina Gina pushes.

"No, if that man wanted my number, he would've asked for it!"

"So! You can still give it to him!" Mia is really arguing this.

"Big no for me dawg, that's thirsty and I ain't finna be THAT! Mkay!"

Quickly this escalates and she demands my business card because she knows I always have them. I reach for a card, and I give it to her. *What have I come to!* Mia jets out the door in record time and catches up to him in the parking lot. She says, "This is my friend's card. You should call her." She strolls back in the door and returns to her seat. I am now mortified. *That was too much, but to my defense she made me. She yelled at me for goodness' sake. He probably won't call anyway.* As the night progresses, I realize I did just get off bedrest and it's likely I came out prematurely.

As I awaken, I'm sicker. I think I have an infection. I rush to try to make it to my appointment to apply for a filler job I should've never applied to in the first place. I end up failing something I could do as second nature. I don't take failing lightly because it's usually a foreign concept. I start to get upset, but it hits me that God wasn't allowing it because it wasn't for me and would not have been worth the opportunity cost. I was supposed to be trusting and obeying, but I called myself making a back-up plan. *Abraham didn't search for a ram, God provided one. Duh to me.* On the drive back home, it became more and more apparent to me that all the plans I was making just might not be His plan. I always end up paying the price when I do it my way. Kelley and I had some troubled water between us for a bit because I stayed too long when He told me to go. Thankfully, this was a quicker lesson. I just happened to learn through embarrassment this time. After a while, I headed to campus for class and decided to kick it at Auntie Cookie's house tonight since I'm still not feeling well. My phone rings and it's an unfamiliar number. I usually ignore them outside of business hours, but something makes me answer.

"Hello."

"Hi, is this Kenny? It's ___." I think this is him. This is the man. I didn't know his name. *I guess that heifa was right.*

"The engineer?"

"Yeah."

I don't quite have my usual privacy, so he agrees to call me later. I wasn't expecting a man who looks like him to look at me, let alone call me.

It's a couple weeks later, the day after my birthday actually. We've been speaking daily even if it's just a quick text. I usually only talk to Jesus and my mom daily, but this feels normal almost, outside of a few jitters at least. I'm with Mia Gina and next thing you know we run into him. He's with his brother and cousins, but he keeps finding his way to me until I leave. Later that night, we talked on the phone until we finally said good night. This is so novel. I suppose if Mia didn't force me to give her my card, I still would've seen him again. We would've had another chance at a meet cute, it's as if we were supposed to meet.

A few days have passed and today we are meeting in person for the first time on purpose. I don't think I'll tire of his voice. He's brilliant and I must admit he's hilarious. He says that not many people make him laugh, but I do. *So it's not just me and Daddy who find me comical. I really am a hoot.* He's also the most handsome man I've ever seen in my life. He tells me that he noticed me as soon as I walked in, he even recalled what I was wearing. He admitted that he debated asking for my number before he walked away, but was impressed I had a card. Though we had both already disclosed a bit via phone, we're able to talk a bit more candidly. He tells me more of why he and his ex-wife divorced and about his children. I tell him that I'm a minister. I divulge that I've never been in a real relationship, but was in a situationship that ended when he had a baby with someone else. I emphasize how important my faith is to me and he shares in it. I tell him about my business plans, and he tells me of his established career. We talk and talk and talk. I feel free to tell him just about anything except the elephant in the room.

> "It's like I've known you for years and can tell you anything," he says looking earnestly into my eyes.

> "Yeah, me too," I say, trying not to be so shy and smitten.

> "You ready to go on this journey?" he asks... *The look on his face I could see everyday, so maybe? I guess I really am ready.*

He walks me to K Scrilla and gives me a proper good night. On the drive home, I'm spent. I'm pretty sure I'm blushing. I won't lie, him being divorced scares me. I'm a product of a divorced couple remarrying and my parents are still married *TUH DIS DAY*. I'm hesitant, but something has me compelled to see where this may go. Though there's an evident age gap, we have so much connecting us. We're so much alike.

It seems we just might be compatible. I see myself beginning to let me guard down *and Ion't like dat.* I don't want to be distracted. I got stuff to do, and I don't see myself telling him about my health right now either. I think it's too soon for that. So far though, I can tell he's supportive and encouraging. It's weird, but our conversation tonight got me thinking it's truly the start of something. Suddenly, I see a whole life in front of me. A few weeks ago the image of a single mom of an adopted daughter seemed like it wasn't so far off, when now I've met a divorced father of two and I might be open to him, even though I'm frightened. This doesn't feel like a casual experience. I'm not in a rush. Feelings can't very well be trusted. It's been over a year since I've been on a single date, but if I'm honest, I don't believe this man is inconsequential to my life like the others. I sense that I'm contemplating more, much more than a date or a little time to spare. This moment feels as if it matters, as if this could profoundly impact my life, *his too*. Even if I don't become his last wife someday, we met for a reason. I just need to know why.

Well, I guess we'll see where it goes. For now, I need to review my day planner, pick out my heels to build an outfit for my pitch tomorrow for a prospective Black Out client, start planning Dope's 2018 calendar, and plan the menu for the new vlog episode for Faith & Food. I jump into grind mode as 'Work To Do' by the Isley Brothers blasts through my stereo.

September 14, 2023

So here's the thing… I'm Kenny, the one who's been living outside of these pages. *If life doesn't turn out how you planned, will you be okay?* I was asked this question throughout the duration of writing. For over seven years, I was being pulled out of the closet of writing for the sake of this collection of words. After countless notes, I heard His voice a bit clearer, and the notes became personal. They became a piece of myself. It required vulnerability. *Let's just say I ain't like that one bit.* Though this was loosely based on my life, my imagination was able to soar. I envisioned ways I would want to live, and I time traveled to years before me, all while trying to live in the now. This was arduous, and it made the query resonate with me more often than I'd even realized. I had no idea how long this process would take, nor could I have prepared for just how personal it would get. When I began living in the years coinciding with this novel, my life certainly did not look like the life I lived in these pages. Truthfully, I began liking the fictitious me more than the real-time me. I began to covet some aspects of that illusory life. *I had to come to grips and repent that.*

Whether fabricated or straight-up, every single word in the book is real in some way. I earned my

Bachelor of Business Administration, operated businesses, worked through grief, experienced terrors and heartaches, felt immense happiness, and had to step into roles not originally meant to cast me while writing each word. I wrote when inspired, sometimes between midnight and 3am while exploring what could and might be. I went through months of writer's block and other times I was too wildly intimidated. Life kept happening as it does -as it will. Real-time changed the abstract future like I was The Flash messing with the speed force. At some points, it seemed as though I lived years in the matter of months, like I disappeared when Thanos snapped his fingers, too. Big life events and the little things altered details of this book, this piece of me.

2019 began with a health scare. Before I fully healed from the surgery, I became the instant mom to a traumatized teen. I legitimately was the 24-year-old guardian of a 17-year-old. I was not okay, but I had an assignment I couldn't refuse or at least I wouldn't refuse. I loved her as my own, as unorthodox as it was. She became my first kid, but it ended. Her no longer being in my family home nearly broke me. On the milestone that was 25, alone I wept over the child who could have never truly been mine. That night I dwelt on how I did not envisage my life to look as it did. There was no obvious forewarning. I thought to myself...*I'm supposed to be happy.* I was supposed to be with my girls or out with somebody's son or something. I was supposed to be celebrating. Now, I'm learning not to wait for a milestone, but to celebrate life every chance I get. *If I'm honest, I haven't really gotten the hang of that yet, not at all really.*

All that year I took hits from my personal life to business to finances to academics. I had to drop clients and went months with no regular income, but God still provided, mainly through my parents. I was depended upon and a dependent all at the same time. My maternal grandmother deteriorated before our eyes, but I had things to do. I had to decide to get okay. It was the first time I ever truly thought I was depressed. It was the only time that phrase ever crossed my lips. I told that to very few people. I was spiritually drained, mentally exhausted, and emotionally depressed. I was not alright, but I had to get up, be the dutiful daughter and granddaughter, be dependable and strong, conduct business and preach and teach the Gospel, while dealing with silent grief and loud anger. I felt far away from God, but still tried to do right by Him. I just kept failing.

Swift changes were occurring nonstop. If I were coming or going, I couldn't tell. Somewhere on the journey of writing in 2017, an unusual curve was thrown. I met a man. A grown man. A real man. I fell in love with him. From the day I met him, it was supernatural. It wasn't who he could become or his potential. It's him, just him, how and who he was and is already. When we met, a man was the furthest thing from my brain. I was focused on staying healthy enough to finish my final senior year of undergrad, building my businesses, and considering dual MBA/JD programs. The day I met him started off with a leap of faith. I picked up my last check from my then main source of income. I needed clients, not a boyfriend. When I locked eyes with him, I promise it was a whole experience. I tried not to make too many plans for my future because I was making God laugh a little too much and a little too hard. I surely never planned on meeting a divorced father of two, but I did. I am a product of a couple who divorced then remarried, so that stayed on my mind. That played on my fears and circumstances only fed the fright, but I tried to move with caution.

Ultimately, time with him began to show me about myself: where I lack and where I overflow, my good, bad, and ugly, but most of all it made me love deeply, sincerely, and unlike I'd ever loved before. I started talking to Jesus on behalf of that man and his children daily. I embraced the sentiment that it's okay to be invested, even if it is scary. It was as if new layers were added to my already layered self. *I'm something like my honey butter biscuits.* The emotions were dangerous for me because I can honestly say that I was so comfortable with being emotionally removed. I was emotionally underdeveloped. God bless that man because he dealt with my newness and me figuring out how to deal with myself. Even after all we experienced, real-life crises, and less than ideal circumstances, I'm happy to have met him, even though the plans we spoke of didn't come to fruition. I accepted that whether with him or alone I still have to live with myself, so I might as well learn to love myself properly.

Meeting him also coincided with struggles in my spirituality. I was entering new levels of my faith and all the things that come with new stages of life. New temptations came. I got saved pretty young so there were some areas I didn't focus on as much because they weren't relevant until they were…

It was difficult coming into new levels while navigating this relationship when what started off so promising hit impasse after impasse. It seemed I was in it by myself, but for the first time in my life I needed someone, not my family and friends, but him. I longed for companionship, understanding, and love. I knew that if I were to be with this man, I would one day be a second wife. *The First Wives Club is one of my favorite movies, so how could this be?!* I never imagined that for myself in the slightest, but then I arrived at a point where I couldn't, rather did not want to, imagine my life without him in it. I wasn't thirsty to be a wife, I believed I would be his wife. I hoped for the honor of being wanted and the beautiful responsibility of being needed by him. Not long after our beginning, our own lives got in the way, namely his. Something terrible happened in his world, my health was out of whack, I became an instant mom, then even more suddenly I was not, I was in a fight for my own stability. It had gotten so dark. I needed him when I could not and that was a bitter pill to swallow. To add insult to injury, I was not allowed to be his place of solace. Understanding circumstances did not make it any easier, but I'm at peace with knowing I tried. *This is not meant to be a cliché perpetuating a woman boiling down her life and value to a man, but it just goes to show how sometimes our plans go out the window.*

Don Michael Corleone loved Appollonia the moment he saw her. It wasn't merely physical attraction nor lust. He loved Kay, but it wasn't like how he'd fallen for Appolonia. I don't ever want to be Kay. *I also don't wanna get blown up in a car, either, but alas.* If I ever have a true love story, I want it to be epic and most of all true.

Sometimes the plan is not only about the results, but the effort. Being with him taught me that, even if it was just on my end. We must be genuine in what we do. We can only control what we do. There are so many external factors that came in and shook ish up, but I was intentional about showing my love even with my flaws. There is no room for anything forced or phony, especially with something so significant.

For someone like me who isn't very in tune with emotions, when I am invested it's concentrated. I was very emotional with him because I was more invested than I've ever been before. I probably wanted us too badly. Maybe God was reminding me to love Him with all my heart, mind, and soul. Maybe He was reminding me to want Him more and acknowledge I need Him more than anyone and anything. I used to repeat that to myself daily as I prayed for us individually and as a unit. I never wanted to forget to keep God first. I didn't want to love this man more than I loved God. I thought I was adamant about checking my heart, but maybe not. Maybe this was just another example that life doesn't go as planned and I gotta buck up and put my big girl panties on and keep on steppin'. I'll always root for the Retired Running Back, he'll always be the Big Shot Engineer to me, even if he's not with me. I pray God pours out favor over him and his children.

When my maternal grandmother passed away in 2020, things shifted again. It hit me that I didn't have to help take care of anyone else right now. I needed to learn to take care of my own needs. For over half my life, I had to help and then I didn't. Regardless of my own health, I'm used to being needed. Not being needed stripped me naked. It was foreign, but the time had come to truly activate independence and live my own life, so my parents could be free of the burden. It forced me to pivot to expand my focus to not only the man and relationship I knew I wanted, *wondering if it would work out,* but to zoom in on me as the person, not just who I am to everyone else. I learned how to take care of people before I could take care of myself. Being left with myself was an unfamiliar hurdle. I was often left to my own thoughts. *Thank God for being a mind regulator!* I needed to revisit and seek out new things to do for fun and fulfillment, not just income. I needed to be intentional about protecting joy and seeking God's peace. I needed to be faithful and trust God for where He was taking me, even when I didn't think I wanted to go. I needed to understand that whether I were to become that beautiful, unrivaled man's last wife or not, I would still be an individual. My job was to learn to love myself not in relation to being needed, but because I existed. I owe it to my Creator and myself to love me. *The least I can do is try.*

I am on my way to being who I am supposed to be. I am a Black woman trying to be defined as more than strong, but I also have to be who I am in this world. I am indubitably flawed, but I pray I am leading a life that makes God smile. Life hasn't been what I planned, but I surmise today can be even better than I could ever plan if I let it. My problem is that I need things to make sense, but some things just don't and I'm ascertaining that it's okay. When I die, I pray I make it. I want to hear "well done." I can only hope that I led some people to Jesus, made some folks feel good, made some laugh, and righted some wrongs. Whether my company blows up and takes me and my heels to great places, there's one thing I'm certain – if I truly relinquish my plan to God, I will be more than okay, even in the moments when I'm very much not. *Cheers!*

My work in real life:

Dope ~ Young NOT Foolish

Black Out ~ Braxton Management

Kenny's Kitchen ~ Kenny's 622 Trowbridge

Food & Faith ~ Kenny's Kitchen Therapy

Braxton Holdings ~ The Don In Heels Inc.

If no one has shown you today, I love you, but my
God loves you better.